Cover Design by Kiersten Modglin
Copy Editing by Three Owls Editing
Proofreading by My Brother's Editor
Formatting by Kiersten Modglin
Copyright © 2022 by Kiersten Modglin.
All rights reserved.

First Print and Electronic Edition: 2022
kierstenmodglinauthor.com

To Becca and Lexy—thanks for making it look like I know what I'm doing.

"The scariest monsters are the ones that lurk within our souls..."

EDGAR ALLAN POE

CHAPTER ONE

BLAKELY

You could scream up here and no one would hear you.

I don't know why it's my first thought as I round the curb that leads to the writing retreat where I'll be spending the next week.

The Victorian house sits high on the hill, the steep gravel driveway enough to make my stomach lurch as I approach it and turn in. It's secluded, as the listing warned, and far steeper than I'm prepared for. My tires skid across the gravel as I mash the accelerator, terrified applying too much pressure might send me over the side of the mountain if I can't stop the car in time.

I suck in a sharp breath as I reach the top and stomp my foot on the brakes, easing in next to the other car in the driveway. From my seat, I take in the sight of the house again.

It's a two-story, brown manor with tall windows, sharp angles, and a three-story tower in the center of the house. There's a steep set of stairs up the hill leading to the front porch. Despite the cost they have listed on their website, the wooden siding could use a good power washing and the weeds are overgrown, making what should be a lush, evergreen Black Hills paradise feel more like a forgotten piece of property.

From where I sit, there's a nearly three-hundred-sixty-degree view of the mountains below us, trees and fog surrounding us for miles.

I flip down my visor to check my reflection and a yellow envelope falls down into my lap. Turning it over, I reread the invitation that brought me here.

Ms. Baldwin,

As one of our favorite authors, you are cordially invited to visit the new Black Hills Manor Writing Retreat. Our mission is to provide writers like yourself a quiet retreat to get away from the craziness of the day to day. Tucked away in the secluded Black Hills of South Dakota, it's the perfect place for you to unwind, find your inspiration, and connect with other writers on similar paths as your own. Our fully stocked retreat comes with everything you could need to relax, unwind, and write your next bestseller—including high-speed Wi-Fi, a loaded pantry, bar, and high-quality toiletries from local vendors right here in the Black Hills; and a hot tub to reset after a long day of writing. We're proud to offer the highest quality mattresses and linens to ensure a restful night's sleep and support the health of your spine.

We hope you'll accept our invitation, and in honor of our launch, we'd like to offer you a FREE week's stay in exchange for a social media post about your experience.

You'll find an email in your inbox further detailing this offer. If you're interested, please respond to the email so we can get you booked for the next available week. Slots are going fast, so please don't delay.

We hope to see you soon!

Yours,

The Team at Black Hills Manor Writing Retreat

I check my reflection and place the invitation back above the visor just as my phone begins vibrating in the seat next to me. I spy my best friend's name on the screen and swipe my thumb across it.

"Hey."

"Hey, just checking in. Have you made it yet?"

"Yeah, I just got here."

"What's it like?"

I stare up at the house. "I haven't gone in yet, but it's beautiful out here."

"I'm glad you made it safely." She's quiet for a moment, then sighs. "Are you sure you're okay to be there this week? I can get Noah to watch Kara if you'd rather go do something else. We could spend the week in a hotel room and eat takeout and watch trashy TV."

I shake my head, though she can't see me, and open my

mouth to respond. My voice catches in my throat. "I need to do this, Katy."

"I know." She sounds sad. Disappointed, maybe. I try not to take it personally. She knows why this is so important in theory, but really, no one understands. How could they?

"Listen, I need to go. I'll call you later, okay?"

"Yeah, okay. Be careful."

"I will."

"Lock your bedroom door at night."

"I will, *Mom*," I tease. "Okay, bye."

As soon as I step from the car, a husky voice greets me.

"Hi there!"

When I spin around, my gaze lands on the man headed in my direction. There's something familiar about him, and I immediately begin to rack my brain for where I might know him from. He's not quite thin, but not quite muscular—somewhere in between—with a dark, full beard and tired eyes. If I had to guess, I'd say he's maybe twenty years older than me, which would put him somewhere in his forties.

"Hi!" I wiggle my fingers with a half wave.

"Welcome."

"Oh. Thank you." I stop at my trunk, grabbing the newly purchased designer luggage from the back. When he draws closer to me, I place the luggage down and extend my hand. "I'm Blakely Baldwin."

He accepts my hand slowly, shaking it, then reaches for my bag. "Daniel Destrange. Here, let me get those. There're a lot of stairs."

Or...at least, he *probably* says something like that.

I don't hear much past his name.

Daniel Destrange?

The Daniel Destrange?

The horror author whose books are on every bestseller chart week in and week out? The one whose books have been adapted to countless movies, whose career I've been following since I was in high school? The writer who inspired me to write my first book? *That* Daniel Destrange?

I study his face, realizing *yes,* it *is* him. I should've known instantly. How could I not? Because I hadn't been expecting to see him here, maybe. Because it makes absolutely no sense that he's here. Or perhaps because he now looks a little more rugged than his headshot would lead you to believe. The beard, for one thing, is new. I've never seen him with anything other than a clean-shaven face. He's also put on some weight, it looks like. His face is now lined with the start of wrinkles, and the longer, unkempt hair isn't something I've seen him sport before. Then again, the headshot on the back of his books is probably as old as I am, and he has no true social media presence. He's one of those tried-and-true, old-school writers. The ones who like to pretend we're all sitting around typewriters with glasses of whiskey and cigars while we create our latest masterpiece.

He does very few signings—most were done early in his career—and even fewer public events. Believe me, I've watched for them. For most of my life, I've dreamed of meeting him, and now, here he is carrying my bags.

Am I hallucinating?

Did I black out?

This has to be a hallucination.

I blink rapidly, trying to wake up.

What if I'm still on the interstate? What if I crash?

I look away from him, closing my trunk as I try to hide my shaking hands. *Jesus, Blakely, pull it together.*

What on earth is he doing here?

This retreat is supposed to be for *regular* writers.

Those of us midlisters lucky enough to occasionally get great placement in a bookstore or national news coverage.

There was no mention of writing royalty.

I'm half tempted to grab my bag from his hands and make a run for it, but I think better of it.

Just breathe.

"Nice to meet you." Just as I'm beginning to feel proud of myself for getting the words out without fumbling them, I slip on the gravel underfoot and nearly fall flat on my face.

Of course I do.

Lucky for me, his hand shoots out and *Daniel Destrange* is suddenly holding me up. Saving my life. Okay, maybe not my life, but you get the picture.

Daniel Destrange's hand is on my arm.

His hand is touching my arm.

My sweaty, unwashed, eighteen-hour-car-ride arm.

I pull myself away from him, my heart pounding in my temples. "S-sorry about that."

"Careful. It's a little slick up here."

I fight against the urge to tell him what a huge fan I am of his work, how he inspired me to start a career of my own. I can't tell him. I won't. He isn't here to be fawned over.

Here, we are peers.

I smooth my hands over my tank top and yoga pants, wishing I'd worn something—anything—better than this, and clear my throat, offering him a small smile as I follow his lead up the stairs.

"So, do you live around here?" He shoots a glance back at me over his shoulder.

"Um, no. I'm from Nashville. Do...do you?"

If he thinks it's strange that I don't know where he lives—or that I'm pretending not to anyway... *I mean, who doesn't have a permanent image of his California mansion plastered in their heads?*—he doesn't remark on it. "I love Nashville. It's a beautiful city." I can hear the smile in his voice without seeing it. "And, to answer your question, no, I'm not from here either. West Coast born and raised."

I nod, though he's no longer looking at me. Suddenly, a thought occurs to me. "Do you... Is this place yours, or are you here for the retreat?"

"No, no. I'm here for the retreat. Same as the rest of you, I'm assuming."

"Are there others here?"

"Two others." We reach the porch and approach the front door. It's made of a white wooden frame surrounding four opaque window panes. He stops long enough to type in a code on the doorknob's keypad. The keys flash green, and I hear a click. Daniel grabs the handle and pushes the door open, and now Daniel Destrange is not only holding my luggage, he's officially opening a door for me. I'm totally dreaming, and I have zero desire to wake up.

"After you."

I step forward into the house. "Thank you."

The entryway is small but leads into a massive open-concept kitchen and living room with tall ceilings and wooden beams running the length of the room. In every direction, through the oversized glass windows, you can see the forest that surrounds us. It's as if we've been swallowed up by wilderness.

Gathered around the granite-topped island to my right are two strangers. They're closer to my age than Daniel's, and I recognize their faces instantly.

The man has a thick head of curly brown hair and smooth, pale skin. His forehead wrinkles as he smiles at me with the kind of casual arrogance that fills up a room. *He's waiting for me to recognize him.* I can see it in his eyes, and though he does look familiar, and I'm sure I know his name, I instantly decide, even if I figure out who he is, I won't let it show.

Luckily for me, I don't have to keep that promise for too long.

"Tennessee Rivers," he says after a moment, trying and failing to hide his disappointment as he extends a hand. "And you're Blakely Baldwin." He tells me this as if I might not know who I am.

"I am." I purse my lips, his name putting a sour taste in my mouth. If I couldn't see the cockiness in his expression, I'd expect it now that I know who he is. Though we've met before in passing at various events, his reputation outshines the vague recollection of my interactions with him.

I read him right.

I turn away from him and toward the woman standing there. She's short, like me, likely around five foot three or four, her skin a warm shade of beige, and she wears her dark hair in a perfectly smooth, chin-length bob. She leans forward over the counter, resting her elbows on the granite.

"You're Lyra James." She's the first one I recognize without question.

She smiles, but it's humble. Unassuming. I like her even more than I did before. "I am. It's nice to meet you."

It hurts that she doesn't recognize me, but I try not to let it show. When I extend my hand, she takes it gently. Her hands are soft and smooth, and even from where I'm standing, I can smell the scent of her citrus perfume. She's the kind of person that makes you feel self-conscious just by existing. Everything about her screams that she has her shit together—a far cry from anything I could claim about myself.

"Yes. It's so good to meet you. Actually, we've met before, though I guess not *officially*. We both spoke at the Southern Authors Conference last year, and we were up for an Edgar the year before. Oh! I came to one of your Nashville signings back in the spring."

"That's right! I knew you looked familiar. Sorry, I go to so many of these things I lose track. And I'm the worst with names. It's nice to see you again, then." Whether or not she's telling the truth, I can't be sure, but I don't care. She's amazing, and I'm maybe even more in awe of her than I am of Daniel, who makes his presence known as he sets my bag down just behind me in order to join us at the island.

"So, we're the only ones here?" I look around.

"So far." Tennessee backs away from the island, turning to pour more coffee into the red mug he's drinking from. "There are five bedrooms, though, so we could be waiting on one more."

"Speaking of, you'd better claim your room before they get here." Lyra juts her chin toward the hall. "There's one more downstairs with me and one more on this floor."

"Oh, uh... I guess I'll take the room downstairs, if that's

okay with you?" I don't know why I ask her, but she nods anyway and points toward the staircase behind me.

"Yep. It's the second door on the left."

I lift my bags, thanking Daniel again as I move toward the staircase. It's dark, hidden in the shadows from the illumination of the windows, but I can see a faint light coming from downstairs.

The carpeted stairs lead me to what feels like a basement. There's definitely concrete under the thin carpet, and to my left, there's an open room with a fireplace and seating on one end of the room and a bar on the other. To my right, there's a hallway with two doors.

I've already forgotten which room she said is mine, but one door is closed—the one Lyra has claimed, I assume—so I step into the room with the open door. It's a good size, with a queen-size bed against the far wall, a private patio outside the sliding glass door to my left, and another fireplace behind me. It also has a private bath, but no television, which lends itself to the whole *escape to focus on writing* thing, but will do nothing for me when I can't sleep tonight.

I drop my bag on the bed with a sigh, so relieved to finally be out of the car, and hear a door slam shut up above me.

The newest arrival.

I check the mirror in my bathroom, running my hands through my hair and swiping the smeared eyeliner from just under my eyes before heading back upstairs.

When I arrive, there's a new woman waiting for me. She looks the closest to my age, maybe even a bit younger, with a larger build. Her auburn-brown hair goes to her midback, with loose curls throughout it. Freckles are splattered across her nose and cheeks, and when she smiles, it's with her full face—eyes crinkling and cheeks growing pink with joy.

"Hi! I'm Aidy!" She rushes toward me, both arms held out for a hug. "It's so nice to meet you. I'm a hugger. I hope you don't mind."

Whether or not I mind, her arms are already around me, so I hug her back. "Nice to meet you, too. I'm Blakely."

"What do you write?" She's still hugging me.

"Domestic thrillers, mostly." I smile as we pull apart, relieved to have someone here who breaks up the tension. It's so rare to find a writer who's an extrovert. "You?"

"Cozies mostly. I tried a psych thriller under a pen name, but that was a disaster." Her laugh is loud and boisterous, as you'd expect. "So, just cozies for me for now. Who knows in the future, though. I swear, I'm all over the place. I'd love to write a fantasy someday. Oh, or a romance, even. What about the rest of you? What do you write?" Her eyes widen and cut to Daniel. "Obviously except you, Mr. Destrange. Gosh, I'm such a huge fan. I read *Anxiety* in college, and it's still one of my all-time favorites."

Daniel shifts uncomfortably despite his smile. "Oh, thank you. Call me Daniel, please."

"And I'm Tennesse Rivers." Tennessee steps up, extending a hand. "I write action thrillers, mostly centered around my protagonist, Humphrey Castro, a former spy who keeps getting dragged back into the field in order to solve the most unsolvable cases in the world."

"Cool." Aidy's response is polite, but her eyes have glazed over just a bit. "And you?"

Lyra smiles. "I write police procedurals."

"Aww, I love that." She bounces up on her tiptoes.

"Gosh, I'm so excited to be here, you guys. Although, I have to admit I'm feeling some impostor syndrome. This place is so pretty and you're all so popular." Her eyes fall on Daniel again. "I'm not totally sure I belong." She walks the length of the room, taking every inch of it in.

"Hey, we all feel that way," I say. "You were invited for a reason."

Her smile is soft and unassuming as her eyes dance over the room.

"It *is* really nice here, though," Tennessee says. "I bet this place cost a fortune. I've been wanting to get a vacation house myself. Something like this would be pretty cool."

We ignore him, each of us staring around the space in awe. It's my first chance to really take in the room, so I follow behind Aidy, eyeing the long, live-edge dining table in the center of the room and the three matching gray couches to my left, tucked beside the wall that belongs to the staircase.

I lift a binder from the tabletop and flip through it, finding coupons for local restaurants and instructions for how to work the remotes, air and heat, and various appliances throughout the house.

The last page is a letter from the owner of the property. I lay the binder flat, trailing a finger across the page protector.

"What's that?" Lyra asks.

"A letter."

"From?" Tennessee moves around behind me, leaning so close I can smell his cologne as he reads it aloud. "'Welcome to the Black Hills Manor Writing Retreat, a peaceful writing retreat conveniently located in the Black Hills of South Dakota. This stunning five-bedroom Victorian manor is steeped in local history and has everything you need for rest, relaxation, and the perfect environment to get away and finally finish that novel."

He pauses to catch his breath before continuing. "The unit comes with self-check-in, laptop-friendly workspaces, and a fully stocked pantry and bar. During your stay, you can unwind in our cozy hot tub or relax on your therapeutic mattresses. In fact, each room is equipped with its own private bathroom and indoor fireplace, so you can choose to never leave your room, if that's your style. Or, if you need to get a bit of inspiration from your surroundings, our retreat is within driving distance of several popular national parks, coffee shops, and wineries. An ideal base to explore all that the Black Hills have to offer, reconnect with nature, and write your first—or next—bestseller."

He sighs, bobbing his head from one side to the other as his voice grows tired and bored. "If you have any issues at all, don't hesitate to reach out via email, or call or visit our main office at the clubhouse, which is located just half a mile away if you cut through the woods behind the house, or, if you prefer to drive, you can find it by taking a right out of the driveway like you're returning to town, turning right on Sycamore Drive two miles past Mitchellsville Store, and then take another right on Birch Drive. The clubhouse amenities include an in-ground pool, two pool tables, various board and card games, and a bar (BYO drinks and food). Everything is available on a first-come, first-served basis. There's a sign out front. GPS isn't reliable up here, so if you need further instructions, please don't hesitate to reach out. More than anything, we want to ensure your stay with us is everything you could dream of.'"

He glances up at us, wariness drawing a line across his forehead. "Sounds like paradise, eh?"

Daniel chuckles under his breath.

"So, what's everyone working on while we're here?" Aidy changes the subject, plopping down onto one of the couches, her hands smoothing the skirt of the dress she's wearing. It's not until that moment I realize it's printed with cacti.

"I'm finishing up edits on my new one," Daniel answers first. "I've been procrastinating for months now, so when the invitation to this place came in, my wife all but shoved me out of the house."

Aidy's giggle is piercing, and her nose wrinkles while her hands grip her skirt. "So, you still procrastinate, after all this time? I've been wondering when I'd finally stop that."

Daniel's smile is patronizing as he moves around the island toward the coffeepot. "I'm afraid, if my career is any indication, it's an important part of every writer's personality."

Again, she giggles, but this time, she covers her mouth and her eyes cut to me. "What about you?"

"Oh, I'm trying to finally make some progress on my newest book. I've pushed my deadline back about four times now."

"See," Daniel teases from behind me.

I turn to give him a grin and meet Lyra's eyes. "What about you, Lyra? What are you working on?"

"Plotting, mostly. I'm starting a new story soon."

"Me too." Tennessee steps toward her, as if it's a bonding moment, obviously irritated that he's last to be asked.

"Well, on that note, I think I'll go take a nap before the work begins." Daniel inhales deeply over his mug of coffee.

"Yeah, I should too." Lyra moves around the corner and toward the stairs. "I'm still jet-lagged from the flight."

Aidy's disappointed. It's written all over her face, but she stands anyway. "Okay, well, I guess I'll unpack then. Where is my room, by the way?" She moves toward her bag and grips the handle.

"Uh, it's down the hall. Last one that's left," Tennessee tells her.

Her eyes follow Daniel as he moves toward the stairs. Finally seeming to come out of a trance, she blinks and shakes her head, hoisting her bag over her arm as she turns her attention back to the rest of us. "Cool. Which way?"

Tennessee gestures down the hall. "Mine's the first one you'll come to. Empty one's next."

"Thanks." She does some sort of bendy thing that looks like a curtsy and disappears down the hall in a rush.

With just the two of us left, Tennessee looks at me, brows lifted with an aloof expression. "Should be an interesting week."

I smile, fighting down the anxiety I already feel. For me, this week is too important for anything to go wrong, but I can't say that. So, instead, I grab one of the apples in the bowl on the counter and take a bite as I head for the stairs.

Here goes nothing.

CHAPTER TWO

BLAKELY

The sound comes from above my head.

Reeeee pft.

I glance up and adjust in bed, trying to decipher what it might've been. Soon enough, I hear it again. It's a scooting of sorts, as if someone is rearranging the furniture in the living room on the main floor.

I tug the covers away from my legs and stand from the bed, moving across the room with an overwhelming curiosity. You could also call it procrastination, if you wanted to get right down to it, but I won't.

It's the first night, after all. I have time.

Besides, I thought there was no one left in the living room upstairs, but that's exactly where the sound seems to be coming from.

Earlier this evening, Daniel prepared everyone a light dinner of caprese salad, and afterward, we all separated to our rooms for a few hours of work before bed. Now I can't help wondering if they've reconvened, and if so, I don't want to miss out.

That's what this experience is all about, after all.

Meeting people.

Enjoying myself.

Getting my mind off of everything so I can focus on this story.

I open the door, noticing Lyra's door is still closed. Is she still working or has she already gone upstairs? I try not to be offended at the possibility of being left out. No one here has any reason to exclude me. It's just my anxiety talking.

There's a faint light from the main level, but I hear no voices as I make my way up. As my foot hits the last step, I hear a sound I'm all too familiar with.

Typing.

Fingers flying across a keyboard at a speed that makes me jealous. I have no idea when I last wrote like that, but I can practically feel the high of it. It's contagious—the best feeling in the world.

The typing stops and I realize they must've heard me, so I step around the corner so I can see into the living room and find Tennessee staring up at me from the couch in front of the window. His face is hidden in the shadows of the room, a single lamp and his computer screen the only things illuminating the space.

"Hey," I say, breaking the silence as I move toward the kitchen island. I don't know what I'm doing other than trying —and failing—not to be awkward, until I open a cabinet and retrieve a wineglass. *Reasonable enough excuse to be up here. Sure.*

"Hey." He returns to his work, fingers flying almost

immediately as I run my hand across the bottles of unopened wine in the stocked wine fridge.

I choose a chardonnay, one of the few I'm familiar with, and fill my glass, then head back for the stairs.

"You don't have to run off, you know." His voice catches me by surprise, and I stop.

"I don't want to bother you. I just needed a drink."

"If I didn't want to be bothered, I'd be in my room." He doesn't look up at me, but his fingers have stopped. "This is a common area. You're welcome to join me. Bring your laptop and work, if you'd like. This view has to beat the one in your room."

For just a moment, I think he's talking about the view of him—the cockiness would be rather on-brand for him—but I quickly realize he's talking about the window behind him when he cuts a glance toward it.

He's not wrong.

Outside the window, it's mostly dark, though the moon is illuminating the woods in a slightly eerie, almost hypnotic way. I picture myself walking outside, slipping into the darkness, and disappearing once and for all.

A corner of his mouth upturns. "Good for inspiration, hmm?"

I clear my throat, looking away. I don't want to spend my evening with him, but I also don't really want to be alone. And I don't want to be rude.

So, I hear myself saying, "Are you sure I won't bother you?"

"Not unless you're one of those writers who blasts music while you write."

To that, I laugh. "Not at all. I prefer silence."

"Well, then, join me." His eyes meet mine for the first time and a chill runs over me, despite the warmth in my belly from my first sip of wine.

"Okay. Um, I'll be right back." I nearly set my glass down, but think better of it. I may have never been a partier like some of my friends, but I know enough not to leave my drink with a stranger unattended. The move doesn't go unnoticed, something that makes me feel both guilty and embarrassed, but he doesn't say anything. Instead, he returns to his work and I hurry down the stairs, spilling a bit of wine as I go.

When I return, he hardly looks up, so I sink onto the couch across from him, place my drink down on an end table, prop my feet up on the coffee table, and open my laptop.

We work silently for a while, his quick typing igniting my competitive nature, keeping me working faster than I have in ages.

I'm so deeply invested in my story, in fact, that it takes me several minutes to realize he's stopped typing altogether and is staring across the room in intense concentration.

Stuck on a plot point, most likely, is my first thought. Then, he looks at me.

"You're from Tennessee, right?"

I nod, wondering how he can say his own name with a straight face. "Nashville, yeah. Why?"

"What brought you all the way out here?"

"Um..." I glance around, as if he's lost his mind. Maybe he has. "A writing retreat. Same as you."

He's still for a moment, then releases a chuckle. "Well, obviously. I meant why *here* specifically. I assume there are mountains in Tennessee."

"You'd assume correctly." My voice comes out stiffer and more defensive than I mean for it to. What is his problem? "Are you trying to get me to leave or something?"

His brows crash together. "What? *No.* No, of course not. I was just... Sorry." He adjusts in his seat, leaning forward over his laptop. "I was just trying to make conversation."

I rebound quickly, my tone lighter as my cheeks flame. "Oh. Well, truth be told, when the invitation came, I thought it was ridiculous to travel so far. But... I needed a getaway." I almost say more, almost tell him why, but I bite my tongue. "What about you? You never said where you're from. Tennessee, I'm assuming?"

"Actually, no. I live in Denver."

I snort. "Well then, why are *you* here? Are you telling me there are no mountains in Colorado?"

He smirks. "Touché. There are plenty of mountains, but I'm actually from here. My mom lives in Spearfish, so this trip was a good chance to come home and see her too."

It's hard to picture Tennessee with a mom, as ridiculous as that sounds. He seems like the kind of man who was never really a child. As if he might've just shot up out of the earth, sporting a cocky grin and giving orders.

"Is that funny?"

I wipe my grin from my face. "Sorry, no. I was...somewhere else. It's nice that you're getting to visit her."

"Thanks." He turns his attention back to his computer, and I think for a moment the conversation is over, but then he comes back with, "What about you? Any family?"

"Um, yeah. I still have my dad and my sisters."

"Sisters? How many?"

"Three." I lean forward, lifting my wineglass from the table and to my lips. "What about you? Any siblings?"

"Yeah, I have two sisters, actually, and our mom."

"Are you all close?"

"We are, yeah. My sisters and I have gotten closer as I've gotten older. I was the baby of the family, so I've always been close to Mom. She's..." His smile is wistful, and finally, I see a side of him I haven't before. "She's a firecracker."

"I'd expect nothing less." I take another sip of wine, relishing the warmth of the drink and our conversation. If you'd have told me an hour ago that I'd be enjoying a conversation with Tennessee Rivers, I'd have called you crazy, but here we are. "So, why Denver? Why'd you leave?"

"I just... I guess I wanted more, you know? A city. Things to do. People."

"And now you're back here to get away from all that."

It's not a question, but he nods anyway. "Same as you."

"Well, I think it's great that—" I pause, something catching my eye over his shoulder beyond the glass.

He follows my gaze as I move to stand, placing my glass and the laptop down. Before I can reach the window, he's up and looking out.

"What the..."

He sees it too, so I'm not dreaming or imagining. This is no trick of light. No hallucination.

Someone is out in the woods.

Just a few feet from the cabin.

The beam of the flashlight is still. They aren't moving. Just standing and...watching?

I don't know. I can't see them.

"Is someone out there?" I whisper, though I don't know

why I feel like I should keep my voice low. It's not as if they could hear me.

"I..."

Before he can answer, before we've even registered what's happening, the light flicks off.

We can't see them anymore.

There's no clue as to who they are or what they're doing out in the woods so late at night. There are no houses nearby, as far as I can tell.

Tennessee glances at the lamp beside him. When he looks back at me, he swallows, and his next words send chills down my spine.

"They could see us watching them."

CHAPTER THREE

LESSA

BEFORE

I study his dark eyes as he walks past me, taking in the way they avoid meeting mine. His scruffy, chestnut hair is carefully tucked behind both ears, his muscles bulging under the thin cotton of his gray T-shirt as he all but struts across the room. He's handsome in an unassuming way, like he knows it but doesn't care if anyone else does.

If he's trying to catch my attention, it's worked. I can hardly look away.

"Excuse me." I raise a finger into the air, calling his eyes to meet mine finally, and when they do, the bolt of lightning that shoots through me is enough to make my knees weak. *Jesus.* That smolder could light a fire.

"Yeah?" He practically grunts it at me.

"I wondered if you could help zip me up?" I pull my hair to the side, though it's not necessary, and step toward him, taking my time turning away to reveal the back of my dress—

the zippered opening exposing me bare down to the base of my spine.

In the mirror, I watch him swallow, his gaze passing over me without pause, before bouncing back up to meet my eyes in the reflection. "Please?" I prompt.

He takes a quick step toward me. "Uh, sure."

"Thanks."

I hold my breath. Despite his confidence just seconds ago, he hesitates before reaching out, but once he does, his hands are steady and sure against the zipper, his knuckles against my skin lighting every inch of me on fire.

This isn't his first rodeo—the man knows what he's doing. I assumed it before, because of the intensity of his gaze, the sharp cut of his jaw. But I'm positive now. His hands are too confident against me. His skin lingers on mine even once he's finished with the zipper.

I swallow and drop my hair, not breaking eye contact.

He doesn't either.

I force a meek smile, though I feel anything but meek right now.

I know what I want, and it's him.

"It looks nice." His gaze flicks down to the dress again, and when I turn around, it remains on the low-cut neckline.

"You think?" I trace a finger across the silk of the dress, where the fabric meets the skin of my chest.

"Mm-hmm." He swallows, looking back up at me. "I mean, I wouldn't wear it to church or nothin', but for a night out..." His head weighs to the side with apparent apprecia-tion, and my cheeks flame.

"It's for another of my parents' stupid parties."

"Your parents?"

He doesn't know.

The realization slams into my chest.

He has no idea who I am.

In this town, that's almost impossible. Now I understand why he wasn't looking at me.

At least, I sort of understand.

I mean, I look damn good in this dress, so it's a shame he hadn't noticed me, but I can forgive that. To him, I'm just a regular girl in a dress shop.

My lips curve into a smile. "Yeah, but anyway, I haven't had dinner yet. What are you doing right now?"

He checks over his shoulder with a mischievous look in his eyes. "I'm...uh, nothing, actually. I'm not doing nothin' that can't wait."

"Good. Then you're taking me to dinner." I press up on my tiptoes with delight.

"Seriously?"

"Are you going to make me second-guess myself?"

He runs a hand through his messy hair and releases a puff of air from his lips. "Nope, guess not. Let's go."

"Attaboy." I pat his chest. "Oh, but I just need to change first. Give me three minutes."

It's less than that before I'm out of the dressing room and making my way toward the counter. I pay for the dress with a swipe of my credit card. He doesn't offer to hold the bag for me, but he does hold the door on our way out, so he's got one thing going for him when he asks, "So, where ya wanna go?"

"I know a place." I grab his hand and dart across the street without looking both ways. *Shame, shame.* That's half the fun, though, isn't it? Being young and carefree. My days of being able to act without thinking are limited. I'll be twenty-eight this year, as my parents like to remind me. Apparently, it's time to get settled down. Time to start figuring some things out.

But, at least for tonight, I have no use for that advice.

For tonight, I want to be fun and free with him.

It takes us about twenty minutes to walk the ten blocks to my favorite restaurant. He stops us in front of it, shifting in place as he squints up at the sign.

"Something wrong?"

"Yeah, I'm not really feeling this place. You sure we can't go somewhere else? There's a place down the street that has good pizza." He juts his chin in the opposite direction, and my mind fills with images of some dingy hole-in-the-wall I'd never be caught dead in.

"That's okay. I'm sure they could make you a pizza here, if that's what you want."

His jaw tenses and he looks up at the sign again, refusing to meet my eyes. "It's just...this place looks..." He rubs his thumb against his fingers, whistling to indicate the place might be expensive, which it is.

Relief spreads through me. "Oh. Is that what this is about?"

"Look, I'm not trying to act like I'm some rich boy like I'm sure you're used to. Do I look like I can afford a place like this?" He gestures toward the building and then toward himself. He's right. He doesn't fit in here, not in this place, not in my world, but that only makes me want him here more. My guess is he doesn't even own a dinner jacket—definitely doesn't have it with him if he does—but they won't press the issue for me like they would for anyone else.

I smile, shaking my head. "Don't worry about it. Come on."

When I take a step back, moving toward the glass front door, he shakes his head. "Nuh-uh, forget that. I'm not some little bitch who's about to let you pay for my dinner."

Before he can say anything else, the door opens and the maître d' greets me by name, "Evening, Ms. Astor."

I hold out a hand, waiting for him to take it, and he shakes his head again. "Come on. Please. For me." I bat my eyelashes at him. "I'll let you make it up to me later."

He swallows, eyes bouncing back and forth between me and the man dressed in a suit, who's still waiting for us to make a decision.

Finally, he places his hand in mine with a groan and a roll of his eyes. We're led inside and seated at a table near the back. The restaurant is alive with the steady hum of quiet conversation and the trill of wineglasses being refilled. The low lighting and live piano being played at the front of the house only add to the ambience.

Once we put in our drink orders and begin to look over the menus, I sense that the way he's looking at me has changed. There's something almost...suspicious in his eyes.

This I'm not used to.

"What?" I offer a small laugh.

"Your last name is Astor? As in..."

So, he didn't miss the way I was greeted, after all. I was hoping he had.

"Yes." I don't elaborate. "As in..." There's no need to finish the sentence. We both understand where we're at now. Only he can decide where we go from here.

He nods slowly, then leans back in his chair. As he does,

he clicks his tongue, the cockiness from earlier returning. "Your daddy wouldn't like you being out with me tonight." There's a challenge in his words that I don't miss.

"Well... My daddy's not here, is he?" I wink as our drinks arrive at the table and lift mine to him, waiting to see what he'll do. His drink is filled after mine, and the waitress places the bottle into the metal ice bucket.

We hardly notice her waiting to take our order as he taps his glass against mine. I get the strange sense he now sees me as a challenge, but he's already won and he has no idea.

For the rest of the evening, any sign of tension is gone, replaced by alcohol and laughter, and I know I made the right decision.

He's not like other men. Not the men in my world anyway.

He's exactly what I need.

CHAPTER FOUR

BLAKELY

PRESENT DAY

As quickly as the light goes out, the fun and carefree tone of our conversation has been wiped away as easily as chalk on a chalkboard, and it is replaced with an unsettling feeling deep in my gut.

"Who would be out in the woods in the middle of the night? Way out here?" I ask.

"I have no idea... Could it have been a trail camera or something? Maybe an animal walked by? Do they have lights?"

"I'm not sure." I watch the woods with laser focus, waiting for the light to reappear. "Maybe it was someone at the office. Or a motion-detecting light there. The letter you read earlier said it's nearby, didn't it?"

"Somewhere out here, yeah. Could it be one of the others? Maybe they went for a walk to clear their head or something?"

A shiver slips down my spine and I run both hands over my arms, trying to ease the goose bumps that have formed. "Maybe. I'm...I'm sure there's a reasonable explanation," I say finally. "Probably nothing to worry about." When in doubt, avoid and deny. That should be my life motto, really. Maybe I'll get it embroidered on a throw pillow.

It doesn't take long after that for Tennessee to excuse himself with a yawn, saying he's going to call it a night, and I follow his lead. I down the rest of my wine on the way into the kitchen and place the glass in the dishwasher.

On the way downstairs, I try not to focus on what happened, I really do. I try not to obsess over every sound the house makes or every crack I hear beyond the sliding glass door in my room.

I squeeze my eyes shut and beg for sleep, despite my growing panic-induced headache. I'm overthinking things, like always. It's what I do. Guess I need that on a throw pillow, too.

I think of my grandma's house, of the pillows with random sayings on them. The memory is foggy as I try to recall what a single one of them said. Maybe one had something to do with dessert?

When all else fails, I take two pain pills and thankfully, that does the trick, easing the pain just enough to let me drift off an hour before sunrise.

THE NEXT MORNING, I wake to the smell of fried food. Bacon, I'd guess. A wave of nausea passes over me, a result of the hangover the glasses of wine at dinner and before bed, combined with the pain pills have given me. I make a mental note to eat more and drink less today.

In the bathroom, I strip out of my pajamas and take a quick shower. The water is refreshing, and without planning to, I stand under it until it runs cold, trying to wake up. Once out of the shower, I put on fresh clothes and push my wet hair back away from my face with a headband. I take my daily multivitamin, more pain medicine to stave off the dull ache already forming at the base of my skull, and the rest of my medications, then I brush my teeth and head upstairs.

There, I find my four housemates already together. Daniel is dressed in sweatpants and a matching gray T-shirt, so he looks more like an inmate than the king of horror that he is. When he catches me staring, he offers a kind smile.

"Morning."

"Morning," he says, placing the plate of bacon on the counter. "Hungry? Breakfast is served."

All at once, the group is up and in the kitchen, reaching for plates, grabbing handfuls of bacon and sausage, scooping eggs, smothering jam onto biscuits, and pouring glasses of orange juice. Lyra adds prosecco to hers before passing the bottle to Aidy when she's done.

"This looks delicious, Daniel. You didn't have to cook for us again."

He shrugs, grabbing a napkin as he makes his way to the table. "Eh, I don't mind. We can all take turns with the rest of the meals, though. Once I get deep into my edits, I'll be pretty useless around here."

"Well," Lyra adds, "there's a ton of food in there that we shouldn't let go to waste. Taking turns is a good idea."

I take a seat next to them. "Well, I'm happy to cook dinner, then. Or lunch. Or both... Whichever."

"Same," Tennessee offers. "I'll do one or the other."

Lyra smears butter on her toast. "Awesome, so Blakely can make lunch, Tennessee will do dinner, then Aidy and I can do breakfast and lunch tomorrow, and we'll just rotate. Daniel can skip his next turn since he's already done two, so Blakely will be back up for dinner tomorrow. And we can always skip if we decide to take a night off or go out or something."

"Easy enough." I dust crumbs from my fingertips.

"How did everyone sleep last night?" Aidy asks, adjusting the strap of her purple suede overalls. "My bed is heavenly."

"Yeah, mine's nice, too." Daniel bites into his biscuit.

I hardly noticed mine, so I don't jump in, but the conversation quickly shifts as Tennessee speaks again.

"So, I think I might try to find the clubhouse today. Anyone else want to come with? They said it's just through the woods, right?"

"What for?" Lyra's brows draw down.

"I don't know. I thought it would be good to know where the office is. Just in case." His eyes flick to me, but are gone just as fast.

"Sure. I'll go with you," Aidy offers.

"Alright, cool. Anyone else?" Again, his eyes land on me, but I look down.

Nope. Not happening.

"I should spend the day working," Daniel says. "But let me know how it is, if you go."

"Yeah, same," Lyra says. "If I start off the day by putting off work, I'll get nothing done."

"Same." I nod. It's true, but it's not why I don't want to go. I don't want to go because I know why Tennessee does. He wants to go to the office so we can find out which direction it's in. See if the light we saw last night might've come from someone there. I suppose I should want to go, too, but I don't.

Maybe it sounds silly, but I'd rather not know.

Avoidance and denial, remember?

If it wasn't from the office, what does that leave? Not a hallucination because Tennessee saw it, too. A trespasser? Maybe, but since we all survived the night, I'm assuming they meant us no harm.

Either way, I'd rather just forget it happened and chalk it up to something strange and unexplained than to search for answers we may not like. If, for example, it was a trespasser, would we feel less safe? Would I want to leave early?

No. It's better this way. I'm just here to find my focus and get my book done. Anything else is a distraction.

"Alright, no big deal. I'll just check it out later, then." He nods at Aidy. "Maybe we can go this afternoon. They're probably right, we should get some work done this morning."

Her smile falters slightly. "Right. No problem. Just let me know."

The rest of breakfast is filled with casual small talk, and before too long, our plates are cleared. I offer to do the dishes while Daniel puts the leftovers away and everyone else disappears to their rooms to get their day started.

"It's nice, isn't it?" Daniel asks in the silence. "The quiet up here. Like nothing I've ever heard."

I smile at him over my shoulder. "It is, yeah. Beautiful."

"There's a family of deer living under the porch. They were outside when I had my coffee on the deck. Used to people, seems like. They just stood there and ate. Weren't bothered by me in the slightest." He closes the refrigerator, moving to stand next to me as I wash the dishes.

"The listing mentioned that there is a lot of local wildlife. Let's just hope they're all as friendly as the deer." I chuckle.

Suddenly, there are footsteps rushing toward us from downstairs.

"Has anyone seen my notes?"

I spin halfway around, keeping my hands in the sink so I don't drip water on the floor. Lyra stands there, her chest rising and falling with heavy breaths.

"Your notes?" Daniel asks.

"My notes for my story. They're in a green notebook. They were lying on my bed this morning, and now they're gone." Her eyes fall to me, an accusation in them.

I was the last to be near her room. Maybe the only one with access to it.

"No," I say quickly. "I haven't seen them. Did you look all over your room? Maybe they fell off the bed somehow?"

She looks unamused, her lips pressed into a thin line. "How would that have happened?"

"I'm not sure... I, um, I mean, I didn't take them, if that's what you're insinuating. They have to be somewhere."

"I'm sure they are," Daniel agrees. "Sometimes it just takes a second set of eyes. Let's go look together." He moves toward her and she backs up slowly, eyes still locked on me until he puts an arm up to get her to turn around. They disappear down the steps and I suck in a breath, trying to listen. I run through everything I did this morning—I know I didn't take them, so why do I suddenly feel so guilty? Moments later, they return empty-handed.

"Did you find them?" I'm almost afraid to ask.

"No. They aren't down there." Her tone is flat. Angry. "Like I said."

"Your door was shut when I came up," I tell her. "I have no idea what could've happened to them. They have to be somewhere."

Giving me the side-eye, she slips past the island, toward the sliding glass door, and out onto the patio.

Great. Day two and, already, I have an enemy.

I cast an embarrassed glance Daniel's way, and he presses his lips into a tight, awkward smile. "I'm sure they'll turn up."

I nod halfheartedly. "They couldn't have just vanished."

"Stranger things've happened." With a shrug of one shoulder, he grabs an apple from the basket in the center of the island, takes a bite out of it, and jogs up the stairs. Releasing a heavy sigh, I return to the dishes.

An hour later, Lyra still hasn't come inside.

I want to talk to her, to explain myself better, but I think no matter what I say right now, it'll only make me look guiltier. It's better to let her calm down and realize she's not being fair. If I give her space, surely things will blow over. With that hope in mind, I head back to my room, planning to get back to work.

Within minutes of settling into my room, I hear her return to her bedroom.

I stiffen, listening closely.

Was she just waiting for me to leave so she could come back inside? Maybe she's feeling as awkward as I am about our interaction, especially that it happened in front of Daniel.

As much as I want to forget it happened, I also want to make it right. Maybe now's my chance to talk to her without an audience, or to offer my help in the search.

I stand, dread filling my stomach as I move from my room toward hers. I knock on the door hesitantly, before I can talk myself out of it.

I can hear her moving around beyond the door, though I'm met with no answer. The heat kicks off, drowning me in pure silence. It's so quiet, I'm sure she can hear my nervous swallow through the wood of the door.

"Lyra?"

Still, there's nothing.

"Hey, it's...it's Blakely. Listen, I'm really sorry about your notes. Could I come help you look? I know I'm the worst about overlooking things and—well, not that you're over-looking anything. I just mean...you know, sometimes two sets of eyes are better than one, like Daniel said. And maybe three sets of eyes are the best and, er, well... I don't know what I'm trying to say." I pause, sucking in a breath. I'm butchering this. Part of me—a stubborn, prideful part—wants to say I don't care. That, reasonably, I know I have nothing to feel guilty about and it isn't my fault she misplaced her note-book. A bigger part of me, though, wants to be her friend. Or, at least, not her enemy. I admire Lyra; I have my entire career. She's done what so many dream of—built the kind of career so many of us aspire to. Our industry isn't huge, though it may seem like it from the outside, and I have no desire to have any enemies, especially not ones I wholeheartedly respect and admire. I just need this problem fixed. I need her to assure me we're good.

God, I feel so needy.

What is wrong with me?

I puff out a breath. "I just hope you know I'd never take your notebook. Or anything else for that matter. Truly. I'm such a huge fan and you inspire me, and—"

"What are you doing?"

It's the right voice, but it comes from the wrong direction.

I spin around, spying Lyra standing behind me, and my stomach flips. How long has she been standing there? Listening to my embarrassing pseudo-apology.

"I..." My face heats with embarrassment, and I point to her door slowly. "I thought..."

She raises a brow, waiting for an answer. Her eyes are pinched at the corners, her lips drawn into a thin line. "Thought what?"

"I'm sorry. I thought you were in your room. I heard...er, I thought I heard someone in there."

What did I hear, if not her? Did I imagine it altogether? Could it have been the sound of the heat?

Her eyes widen slightly as she moves past me, pushing open the door and looking around. After a beat, she turns back, shaking her head. "There's no one here."

"Sorry, I... I could've sworn I heard something."

She doesn't respond right away, her eyes scanning the

room again. "Everyone else is upstairs." I can't tell if she believes me.

"Well, maybe it was someone upstairs, then. I'm sorry." *Stop apologizing.* I shove my hands into my pockets.

"I—" She stops, her mouth dropping open as her eyes zero in on something across the room. She hurries toward the bed—no, toward the nightstand—and lifts up a green book.

No. *A notebook.*

Based on the shock written all over her face, I'd guess it's *the* notebook. The one that's supposed to be missing.

She flips it open, confirming that I'm right, then clutches it to her chest. Suddenly, her eyes flick to meet mine.

I don't ask, though I want to. Instead, I fear this makes me look even guiltier.

"Looks like your phantom noisemaker brought my notebook back."

There it is, the confirmation of my worst fears. This further substantiates her suspicion that I took her notebook. *Which I didn't.*

"I'm so glad you found it." My voice sounds weak, even to my own ears, and I feel as if I should say more, but there's nothing to say. My silence makes me look bad, but further denial might make me look worse.

Giving up, I turn, slipping away from her and back into my bedroom. I feel like the main character of one of my books...

If I were writing this scene, what would I have my heroine do? My characters are extensions of myself—better, stronger, smarter versions of me. No doubt, they'd know how to handle this a million times better than I had. But, as it stands, I'm at a loss, and so I decide to do what I do best and ignore it.

We just have a few days left here. It will all blow over eventually. It has to.

I'll keep my head down, get through the week, and move on. After all, I'm not here to make friends. I have work to do.

CHAPTER FIVE

LESSA

BEFORE

"Turn here."

The look on his face changes as we cross the invisible boundary between his side of town and mine. Up until now, every time we've been together, we've gone to his apartment. It's where he's comfortable—fine. And it's where I've been able to understand him better—great. But now it's time to introduce him to my world.

I'll be honest. When this all started, I'm not sure I thought of Paul as a serious prospect. I knew we could have some fun together, but he wasn't exactly my idea of a serious boyfriend. But now, I really do like him. Like, as a person, not just a body.

Which is why this is so important.

"Where are we going again?" His dark, intense brows harden, a look that sends my heart racing.

"You'll see." I wink at him, sticking my tongue through my teeth.

"I already see." He gestures toward the Johnsons' house —half the size of ours—as we drive past it. "I'm guessing you live around here."

I quirk my lips into a smile. "Fair guess."

He stares at me long and hard when we come to a stop at an intersection. "Where are we going, Lessa? Why are we here?"

"I just wanted you to see my place."

"Why? I don't fit in there."

"You fit in with me."

"Sure, anywhere but there. Once you see me there, you're gonna realize this doesn't work."

"Don't be ridiculous. It's just a house." I shrug one shoulder casually.

"It's not just a house. It's a *world*. It's your parents' world. I'm not part of it, and I never will be." He runs his hands over the steering wheel, still not moving us forward.

I understand his hesitation, I really do. I've had numerous boyfriends in the past who were intimidated by my parents, and they all came from this world to begin with. I'm not oblivious to who my parents are or who Paul is, but all that matters to me is that he tries.

"I'm not asking you to be part of it. I'm asking you to spend time with me. Here. In my world. Let me handle my parents."

He grumbles something under his breath and sets his gaze straight ahead, twisting and turning his grip around the steering wheel until an asshole in a red Ferrari screeches to a stop behind us and blares his horn.

I laugh, but Paul doesn't. He's angry. I get it. I should've told him where we were going today. I should prepare him for what's waiting for us, but if I'd given him even the slightest hint, I wouldn't have gotten him this far.

"It's straight up ahead. The end of the cul-de-sac." I point in the general direction of the house as he steps on the accelerator, moving us through the neighborhood at a snail's pace. "Come on. It's going to be fine." It's a promise I shouldn't make and certainly can't keep, and we both know it.

I reach across the console, resting my hand on his thigh as the Ferrari swerves around us, the driver casting a pointed stare that's readable even through the tinted windows. No doubt he's judging the dusty maroon Honda like I would've not so long ago. Probably thinking we're casing the neighborhood or dreaming of a home we'll never be able to afford. Maybe both.

As my house comes into view—an enormous French-style home sitting back behind a gated, circular drive, with plenty of oversized windows, a grand, sweeping staircase leading to the double front doors, and balconies on each end of the top floor—he shakes his head.

"That one?"

"That's the one."

It's a wonder he hasn't seen our home before, honestly. It's been featured in several magazines, and even a film once, but to me, it's always just been the place I grew up. The kitchen where my friends and I made banana-and-honey face masks when we were in high school. The yard where I had lain out to get a tan every summer. The sitting room where my dad drinks his scotch after a particularly hard day.

It all looks pretty from a distance, but I see the cracks no one else does.

"What the hell?" It's a barely audible whisper, and the car slows even more.

Beyond the gate, the lawn is lined with luxury cars and two of the staff members are standing at the end of the driveway. They eye the car dubiously as we grow closer to them.

"It's fine. Just a garden party. We'll be in and out. I promise."

"A garden party? Jesus Christ, I'm in fucking blue jeans, Lessa."

"No one cares," I lie. "I'll get you something new to wear inside if you want, but you look fine."

He doesn't believe me, but it's true. He looks more real than anyone else in attendance. At the end of the street, with nowhere else to go, he slows the car, his cheeks flaming red. He looks like he hates me.

Maybe he does.

One of the staff approaches us apprehensively, and I try to remember how he's shown me to roll my window down.

It's too late, though. Ted, one of Daddy's usual drivers, has already made his way around the car and lowered his face to Paul's window. Paul grips the small crank handle on his door and turns it, lowering the window slowly.

That's how...

"Service members park in the back." Ted points toward the back entrance of the house from the street. "You'll have to turn arou—" When his eyes land on me, he cuts himself off. "Oh. Miss—Miss Astor. I'm so sorry, ma'am. I didn't...um — *Nick.*" He stands straight, waving his coworker over to open my door in an instant, just as he opens Paul's. "I didn't realize. I'm so sorry."

I don't respond, hoping he's learned a lesson in judgment as I step out and move to the front of the car. Paul joins me, adjusting the flannel shirt he's wearing and tugging at the ill-fitting jeans.

I loop my arm through his, if for nothing more than to stop his fidgeting, and smile. We've caught the attention of the people on the lawn or climbing the staircase and, at the top of the staircase, I can see my parents—perfect as a plastic bride and groom atop a wedding cake.

Their grimaces are easy enough to decipher even from where I stand.

My smile grows more genuine by the minute.

Here goes nothing.

CHAPTER SIX

BLAKELY

PRESENT DAY

Everyone is drunk by the time the sun sets. Not stupid or sloppy drunk, but drunk enough that cheeks have flushed red, eyes have glossed over, and words are flowing more freely than they have been.

Perhaps it's because, at this point, we're all just a bit more comfortable with each other. Perhaps it's because there's a sort of collective relief throughout the house, now that Lyra has found her notes and things are somewhat back to normal. Or perhaps it's the opposite—things feel more tense now and we don't know what to do with ourselves.

So, we lean on the society-approved crutch.

The socially acceptable addiction.

We're sitting around the hot tub. Actually, Aidy, Tennessee, and Lyra are inside of it—arms drooping lazily over the sides, hands gripping wine and bourbon glasses—while Daniel and I sit in wicker rocking chairs around it.

The air smells of pine needles and dried leaves, a scent memory that brings me back to hayrides, carving jack-o'-lanterns, and pumpkin patches. Something burns in the back of my throat, a sort of longing for a time so much simpler than this. I swallow it down.

Lyra hasn't mentioned her notes any more today, so at least for the moment, it seems like she's going to let what happened go, and for that, I'm grateful.

Aidy has her phone connected via Bluetooth to the outdoor speakers and she's playing an eclectic range of music —everything from movie soundtracks and Broadway to rap and heavy metal—but the volume is low, just enough that I occasionally catch a word or two. For the most part, it serves as a backdrop to our little party.

That's what this feels like.

A party.

Like we could be friends.

Like maybe we are.

But we're not. We're strangers, trying to pretend we're not if only so this feels somewhat normal.

"So, when did you feel like you'd made it?" Tennessee asks Daniel, swirling the bourbon in his glass with an air of sophistication. "Like, was there one specific moment or..."

Daniel shifts in his seat, his head falling back against the wood of the chair.

If we were sober, I'd feel secondhand embarrassment for them both, and have to fight the urge to interject and assure Daniel he doesn't have to answer.

Instead, I say nothing. I sit and I wait.

Neither of these grown men is my responsibility. Not their comfort or their levels of inebriation.

"I don't know." Daniel tugs at one leg of his pants. "Seeing my books on shelves when I'm not expecting to—in little stores and at the airport—that's been nice."

"Your first movie?" Aidy pushes herself forward in the hot tub, until she's resting against the side closest to us, staring at Daniel with intense focus. At this point, I'm enjoying being surprised by Aidy's eccentric fashion sense as much as anything. Tonight, her bathing suit has tiny pictures of Snoop Dogg on it.

"Also nice." He rubs his finger across his bottom lip. "I think, if I'm being honest, as soon as my first book was published, I felt like I'd made it. And the rest of my life has just been full of moments proving I had no idea what *making it* meant yet. Maybe I still don't."

"Life's too short to get stagnant." Lyra purses her lips, running a hand through the bubbles in front of her. "Feel like you've made it, and you'll stop trying to go further."

"Exactly." Daniel tips his beer toward her appreciatively. "Besides...*modesty is what separates the goods from the greats.* Isn't that right, Blakely?"

I whip my head around to meet his eyes as he gives me a wry smile. I'd recognize that quote anywhere—it's something the main character says in my third book.

"You've read my work?" I'm struggling to catch my breath as I wait for him to nod.

"No way!" Tennessee leans farther toward us, Aidy too, and even Lyra can't hide her shock, but all I see is Daniel. The upturned corners of his mouth, the twinkle in his eyes.

"Once or twice." It's all he says, but it's enough to make me second-guess all my life choices. *He's read my work?* I don't know whether to be flattered or mortified. No one plans for their heroes to scrutinize their work. I don't dare to ask whether he liked them.

Finding out he didn't would shred any morsel of confidence I have left.

"Well, aren't you just the golden girl?" I don't miss Lyra's dry comment, but I can't bring myself to respond.

"Moving on..." Tennessee drags out the words, though he seems to be enjoying the drama of it all. "What do your families think of your books?"

The question cuts straight to my core, an icy palm gripping my spine. He doesn't mean anything by asking, doesn't understand what asking this question does to me, but that truth doesn't stop the immediate ache in my chest.

He's looking at me, waiting for me to answer, but if I dare open my mouth, tears will find me before words.

No. I have to keep it together. Can't let them see me break. Can't ever let them see me break.

Instead, I press my lips together, shifting my gaze toward Aidy, praying someone else will answer.

"My wife reads all my books first and is my biggest fan, hands down. We have two daughters: thirteen and nine." Lyra's response comes after she's taken a sip of her wine, the glass fogged over with steam from the hot tub's heat. "Our oldest is just starting to read my books, but she prefers Colleen Hoover." She snorts.

"How fun!" Aidy slips back into her original seat, eyeing her enthusiastically. "You're so lucky. I want kids someday, but it's just me and my mom right now. She reads all my books, too. I couldn't do this without her."

The wind picks up, carrying with it the fresh scent of the forest, and a chill runs over me. Now that I've regained my composure, I rub a hand over my arm. When Tennessee looks my way, I finally feel prepared to answer. "My family doesn't really read my stuff. My dad's not a reader and my sisters are all busy. My best friend reads all my books early, though."

Even though I thought I was okay, just answering the question has tears burning my eyes, and I take another drink to hide it.

"What about you?" Aidy asks Tennessee, drawing the attention away from me. I could kiss her.

"Uh, well, no wife or kids yet, but I have a niece and two nephews I'm crazy about. They're much, much too young to read my books, though. My mom and my sisters all do, but it's not really their genre, so..." He trails off, then flicks a glance at Daniel. "I can't remember if you have kids or not. I know you've mentioned your wife a few times when I've seen you on panels."

"We have a son. He's in his twenties now, off to college." Daniel's smile is soft and endearing. I don't know why, but I've always pictured him to be more mysterious. Quiet. Harsh. Even as an author myself, sometimes it's hard to separate the creator from the masterpiece.

"Did anyone else get *the talk* about coming here? When I told my mom where we were staying, she called me crazy," Tennessee says with a dry laugh. "Maybe I am, but then again, I guess we all are."

I'm pulled from my thoughts in an instant, just as Aidy asks, "Wait... What do you mean?"

"Well, just, like, with the history of the place, I mean." He shrugs, taking another sip of his bourbon. "Hey, I was thinking for dinner tomorrow we should all go to—"

"History of the place?" That's Daniel, looking every bit as concerned as I feel.

"What are you talking about?" Lyra demands. "What history?"

He's still for a moment, his eyes darting back and forth between the four of us. Then, he stiffens. "Wait, you guys don't know what happened here?"

Chills line my arms, my heart rate increasing.

"*What* happened here?" Daniel's tone is stern. So stern I finally understand where the darkness in his stories comes from.

"Th-there was a murder." Tennessee clears his throat, pushing himself to sit straighter. "I assumed you all knew."

"A murder *here?*" Aidy's cheeks have gone pale.

"When?" All eyes fall to me as I bark out the question.

"Is this some stupid joke?" Lyra looks unimpressed, her deep-maroon lips pursed with irritation.

"No, it's not a joke. Of course not. It happened a long time ago... When I was young. Like, maybe thirtyish years ago? Some dude was killed."

I swallow, blinking slowly to regain my composure. "How do you know? Why wouldn't we have heard about it?"

"I'm sorry. I really didn't mean to upset you. Any of you." He offers an apologetic grimace. "I just assumed you all knew. I thought that was why they only invited writers from our genre to this thing, like they were playing up the history or whatever."

"There was nothing about the history in my invitation." Aidy looks as if she might cry. "If they'd mentioned it, there's no way I would've come. I like fictional, scary stories, but I don't want to live them."

"What happened to him?" Daniel's brows are pinched together, his lips tight. "The man who died."

"I don't know exactly. I think it was a robbery gone wrong. Like...maybe they weren't supposed to be home or maybe it was the middle of the night or something. I can't really remember. I was young, like I said. Too young to really understand or care what happened, but once I started school, there were all these rumors about this place. Everyone always said the house was haunted. Growing up, people would swear they'd hear screams...babies crying... gunshots... They'd see the dude's ghost, all that stuff. By the time I got into high school, the rumors had calmed down. It was kind of old news by then. Most of the adults in town had moved on from it and the house was all but condemned, so we'd sneak out here and use it as a place to hook up or drink or whatever. But it sold last year, and they turned it into this." He held his hands up, gesturing around us. "Kind of clever, I guess. Better than letting it fall in, at least."

"That's...kind of terrible." Aidy's voice was soft.

"She's right. That's disgusting. Profiting off of people's pain is the lowest of low." I wrinkle my nose in disgust. "If I'd known, I never would've come."

Tennessee sighs, resting his chin on his bicep where it lies on the edge of the hot tub. "It was a long time ago. If they hadn't done something with it, it literally would've ended up caving in or being torn down by the city. Bad history or not, this *is* a historic place here. Better to turn it into something than to let it fall apart."

"I'm not sure the family would agree." I shake my head. With a jolt, I realize what I'm doing and loosen my grip on my wineglass. A few more seconds and I may have shattered it.

He shrugs. "Hey, don't look at me. *I* didn't buy it and turn it into this. No one asked my opinion. I'm just saying—"

"Well, don't. I'm not about to sit up here and talk about people being murdered while we're staying in some creepy mansion in the woods. I've seen that horror movie." Lyra pushes out of the water and adjusts the orange straps of her bikini top. "I'm going to bed."

"Wait, you don't have to go. I'll shut up about it."

"It's late anyway. I need to be up early to write." She steps out of the hot tub, setting her wineglass down long enough to wrap a towel around herself before she disappears into the house.

"On that note..." Daniel stands and stretches both hands over his head. "I'm going to try to get a few more hours of work in before it gets too late." He drains the rest of his beer into his mouth and slips through the sliding glass door.

Aidy sits quietly for a while, staring off into the woods surrounding us. The darkness sometimes makes me feel like the world has ended. Like we're all that's left.

I wonder if I'm alone in that or if they feel it too.

"I'm sorry if I scared you," Tennessee says after a moment. He's not looking at either one of us, really. "I honestly thought everyone knew. It was big news in this town. I forget that you're not all from around here."

"It's fine." Her smile is soft and unconvincing. "I get it. But...I should really get back to work too. My best words seem to come after I've had a few drinks."

"Really? With cozies?" Tennessee's brows crash

together. "I guess I always pictured you all sitting around with a mug of tea and a cat rolling around at your feet."

"Well, we have all that too. But it's even better when the tea is spiked." She giggles before standing up to climb over the side of the hot tub, nearly slipping as her foot misses a step. "Oops." She manages to catch herself, wrapping up in a towel as she yawns. "Good night. See you guys in the morning."

Minutes later, she's back inside and it's just Tennessee and I left.

Sounds like a bad country song.

"Are you being serious about the house?" I narrow my gaze at him. "Or is this some sort of sick joke?"

"Why would I joke about that?"

"I don't know. Maybe you think it's funny to scare a bunch of women all alone up here in the middle of nowhere."

His brows draw down, and maybe for the first time, it seems he realizes what he's done and why it's made everyone so uncomfortable. Indignation swells in my stomach and I stand, ready to go inside like everyone else.

His hand darts out to stop me from leaving without warning, gripping my wrist as I pass by the hot tub. I stare down at it, then back up at him.

"What are you doing?"

He leans over the edge, staring up at me from behind hooded eyelids. "I'm sorry." When he releases me, there's a wet ring around my wrist from his palm, and I make a show of drying it off. "I really am. Truly, I wasn't thinking. I honestly thought you knew."

"Even if we did, why would we want to talk about that

right now?" Without the liquor coursing through me, I would never feel comfortable being so bold. "Look, I know guys like you. Guys who try to make everyone around them feel small in order to make themselves feel better. Guys who get off on making everyone around them uncomfortable. Who need to feel dominant in every situation. But it won't work with me. I have no interest in playing whatever game you think this is."

"I..." He shook his head. "Look, Blakely, you've got me all wrong. It's not that I'm trying to scare anyone or make you feel...small or uncomfortable or...whatever else. I just...sometimes I struggle with making small talk. I know I come across as arrogant, but I promise it's not because I'm trying to. I just wanted to fill the silence, and I managed to screw it all up."

I study him, half wanting to believe him, half praying he's been lying about everything. If he's lying, it's easier, because I don't have to care.

Caring is what hurts the most. Caring about someone gives them the chance to destroy you. It's vulnerability in the worst way.

"Why are you so mad, anyway?" he asks, studying me with his head cocked to the side.

"Same reason everyone else is. You made us uncomfortable." I step forward but his arm shoots out again, catching me at the wrist in almost the exact same place.

"No."

"What do you mean *no*?"

"There's something else, isn't there? The others are annoyed or freaked out or whatever, but you're..." It takes him a minute to find the right word. "*Angry*. Why?"

I jerk my arm from his grasp. "Screw you, Tennessee. You don't know me."

"Blakely, wait! Talk to me." His gaze follows my path as I storm away from him and into the house, but to my relief, he doesn't chase after me. When I check over my shoulder before heading downstairs, his dark eyes are still watching through the glass.

You don't know me, I'd screamed at him, but somehow, that's not true. What scares me is that he seems to know me better than most people.

You're angry.

His words echo in my head, pounding against my skull. He'd seen it, understood it, but he didn't know why. Wouldn't. Could never know the truth.

I had to make sure of that. I had to stay *far* away from Tennessee.

CHAPTER SEVEN

LESSA

BEFORE

When I shiver, he drags the blanket up over my legs without looking my way, almost like it's an instinct. Sometimes, I think it is. We're so in tune with each other. We've been dating for just six months, but already, I feel like he's an extension of me. Like he can read my every thought, sense my every need.

Sometimes even before I can.

"Everything okay?" He senses me staring and looks over.

"Mm-hmm." I purse my lips as he leans in to kiss them. "Everything's perfect."

He runs a hand over my hair, settling in with an arm around me as he turns his attention back to the screen.

A knock on the door interrupts us, and he looks over at me again, his brows drawn down.

"Are you expecting someone?" I ask, though I already know the answer based on the expression he wears.

"Not that I know of." He stands and moves across the small living room to peer out of the window. When he turns back to me, something in my gut sinks. "Um... It's the police."

I don't have time to ask more questions before he reaches the door and swings it open. "Officers?"

"Good evening. Are you Paul Brody?"

He shifts, moving to shove a hand in his pocket, but seems to think better of it and lets it fall back down awkwardly. "I...*am*. Can I help you?"

"We're looking for—" The officer's voice halts as I come into view behind Paul. "Miss Astor. I'm glad to see you're okay." There are two of them, one with a thick mustache and thinning hair and the other with broad shoulders and short, buzz-cut orange hair. They study me with odd expressions.

"Why wouldn't I be?" I cock my head to the side and lick my lips, a strange sort of coolness sweeping through me.

The officers exchange glances with one another before the one with a thick mustache clears his throat. "Your parents were..." His eyes fall to Paul for just a moment, but it's long enough to tell me exactly what's going on. "They were worried about you. They asked us to do a welfare check."

My hand falls to my hip instinctually. "And why would they do that?"

"Can you confirm that you're okay, ma'am? Do you...feel unsafe? Are you in any danger? Would you like us to take you home?"

I roll my eyes. "No, I would not. I'm fine. My parents are just trying to get my attention. I'm sorry they wasted your time."

The redheaded officer shifts in place, his hands resting on his hips. "Ma'am, they said you haven't been home in several days. Is that true?"

"Is that any of your business? Or theirs, for that matter? I'm twenty-eight years old. Who exactly am I supposed to be answering to?" My brows crash together as I shake my head in disbelief. When they don't answer, I add, "Yes, I've been staying here *with my boyfriend,* and I'm perfectly fine. You can tell them that." I put a hand on Paul's chest, sidling up against his side.

The officers hesitate, studying me. With a look of apprehension, Mustache finally says, "Do you mind if we just look around?" They're asking me as if it's my place. As if Paul isn't standing right next to me.

"Sure—"

I cut him off before he can give permission. "Actually, we do mind. As I said, I'm an adult. I don't have to answer to my parents. They have no right to butt into my life, and no right to drag anyone else into it either. I appreciate that you're doing your job, officers, but as I've told you, I'm fine. So please, let us enjoy the rest of our evening."

They're silent for a moment, and I meet their unyielding stares with one of my own. Finally, the tension breaks as the redheaded officer takes a step back. "Okay. If you're sure you're okay, we'll leave you to it. We're sorry to have disturbed you, ma'am." No apology is offered to Paul.

I reach for the door and slam it shut, anger swelling in my chest.

He's stone faced and silent, staring straight ahead as their car doors shut outside. He blinks, lowering his gaze to me finally. "What the hell was that about?"

"My parents, trying to prove they still have power over me." I shake my head. "Ignore them. I'm so sorry. I should've known they'd try something like this."

"Why? What did they think was going to happen?"

"Nothing, that's exactly the point. They knew nothing would change. They just wanted to shake us up some." I step forward, resting a hand on his chest again. I'm so close, I can feel his breath on my lips. "Look, I haven't spoken to them since the garden party—"

He scoffs. After being ignored by every one of my parents' guests and basically dismissed from the party, it's a bit of a sore subject.

"I haven't. And I'm sure that upsets them—"

"Upsets, right," he mumbles.

"Yes, *upsets*. But I don't care. I don't care, Paul. Don't you see that? I only care about you. About us." I trace a finger along his neck and over his ear. "We can't escape my parents. Not in this town. Maybe not anywhere. They have power and money and influence, and they're going to use it to try to get me back. That's all they know how to do, and they believe they'll win—"

"*Will* they?" He tilts his head forward slightly, vulnerability in his dark eyes.

"No. They won't. They can't. They'll eventually get bored and move on. For now, we just have to ignore them. It's pathetic, really. I'm nearly thirty years old, and they still treat me like a child."

"Well, maybe you should stop acting like a child."

I suck in a breath. "Excuse me?"

He lowers his head farther, releasing a sigh. "Forget it."

When he goes to walk away, I grab his arm. "No, wait. Tell me. Do you think I act like a child?"

"You still live at home, Lessa. Your parents still pay your bills. You still get an allowance, for Christ's sake."

Indignant tears sting my eyes without warning, and hatred fills my gut—hatred for myself rather than him. He's right. I know he is. But what am I supposed to do? It's not like I can just get a job like a regular person.

I'm not regular.

My parents didn't prepare me for the real world. I'm woman enough to admit that. I have no idea how to get a job, let alone what it'll take to hold one.

Like it or not, it's the reality.

Our reality.

"I have money, Paul. You know that. I have a good life. I've never tried to hide that. But I can get my own place any time I want—"

"So do it."

"I will."

"Good."

He presses his chest into mine, our breaths growing erratic as he searches my eyes. I smirk.

"Besides..." I walk my fingers up the side of his face, flattening my palm across his cheek as I lean in. "I believe we've done some pretty *grown-up* things together, don't you?"

A growl comes from somewhere deep in his throat, a fire spreading to his eyes that I feel in my core.

I grin as I feel his hands gripping my waist.

Just like that, the fight and my parents are all but forgotten. At least for now.

CHAPTER EIGHT

BLAKELY

PRESENT DAY

"What the hell did you all do last night after we went to bed?" I'm hit with the question before I make it to the top of the stairs.

"I'm...sorry?"

Lyra's lips are pursed, one hand on her cocked hip. There's a towel slung over one arm, and I can see the strap of her bikini peeking out from under the T-shirt she's wearing.

"The hot tub isn't working." Aidy, behind Lyra, seems less angry. "The screen won't even come on. We didn't know if something happened last night."

"Um, no. Not that I know of. When I went to bed, it was still working and Tennessee was still in it." There's no way they're going to pin something else on me. "Have you asked him?"

"He's working." Aidy points down the hall. "Door's locked with a *do not disturb* sign taped to it."

At that moment, Daniel appears in the doorway of the sliding glass door, nearly making me shriek from the abruptness of it. He rests both hands on either side of his head against the open frame. "We're going to have to call someone. Whatever the problem is, it's above my pay grade."

Lyra groans loudly. "Thanks for trying." She moves across the room as Daniel steps inside, drying his arms with a kitchen towel. Pulling the home's instructional binder down from the mantel, she flips through it, tapping a long, pink fingernail on the page when she locates the phone number. She dials it into the cell phone in her hand and waits, tapping an impatient finger against the side of her phone.

After several minutes, she pulls it down from her ear with an exaggerated frown. "No answer."

"Maybe you should leave a message." I check the time. "It's still early. Does it say when they open?"

She redials and waits, looking even more agitated, and eventually sighs. "Hi. This is Lyra James. I'm staying at the Black Hills Manor—the, er, writing retreat. And we're having issues with our hot tub. It's not coming on and the water has completely cooled down. We need someone to come take a look at it today, if possible. Give me a call back." She recites her number before hanging up.

We all stare at each other for a few moments, waiting for a returned phone call or a break in the newfound silence. Eventually, Lyra moves past me, back toward the stairs. "I guess I'm going back to work, then."

I wince when her door slams from downstairs a few minutes later and find Aidy's apologetic smile waiting for me.

"Don't worry. She's not mad at you. The coffeepot is being weird this morning, too. She just needs some caffeine."

I frown, wanting to say more. Wanting to tell her that no matter what I do, Lyra seems to hate and blame me, and that I doubt it has very much to do with the coffeepot or the hot tub, though I don't know what it *actually* has to do with. But I don't. I don't say a word about anything, because despite the way she's treated me, Lyra is still someone I look up to, both as a woman and as a titan in my industry. Discussing my frustration with her now will only make things worse.

So, instead, I say, "Something's wrong with the coffeepot? It worked fine yesterday."

From the sink, Daniel calls over his shoulder, "Yeah, it's the strangest thing. It's not coming on either. Almost like something in this wall short-circuited." He gestures toward the wall behind the sink, where the hot tub is also plugged in on the exterior of the house.

"Did it storm last night, maybe?" I ask. "That could explain it."

"Not that I know of."

"Maybe we should ask Tennessee anyway," Aidy says softly, almost as if she regrets the words before she says them. "I know he's busy, but if he knows what might've happened, maybe he knows how to fix it. Or he could at least tell us what we should tell the office."

"Maybe." Daniel grabs a peach from the bowl of fruit and washes it under the sink, reminding me it's my turn to cook breakfast. Shoot. I hadn't meant to oversleep. "For now," he goes on, "I'm going to run into town and pick up some coffee for everyone. Do you need anything?" Daniel looks between us and, when we shake our heads, he turns toward the door, scooping up his keys from the counter.

When the door shuts moments later, Aidy watches me, perhaps to see what I'll decide to do, but I'm not planning to bother Tennessee. After last night, I'd be okay never speaking to him again.

"Well, it wouldn't be a vacation if things didn't go wrong, hmm?" I offer her a small smile, which she returns, though hers seems more distracted than usual. "I guess it's too late for me to cook breakfast. I completely forgot. I'll take lunch duty instead."

"Is everything okay?" she asks, almost abruptly.

"With me? Yeah, why wouldn't it be?" My back is to her as I pull a granola bar from the pantry.

"Just asking... I know everyone seemed kind of freaked out after what he told us last night."

I glance over my shoulder to find her staring off into space, a haunted look in her eyes. "Yeah. It wasn't cool of him to do that, but honestly, I wouldn't worry about it. Don't let him get to you. He just wanted to scare us. It's a game for him."

Her smile is halfhearted; only one corner upturns. "I know. It's just... Creepy, I guess. To consider the possibility that...it happened here."

"He was lying, Aidy. It's not true." I take a bite of my granola bar and shut the cabinet, patting her arm gently as I walk past. "Don't let him get in your head."

I repeat the instructions to myself as I make my way back into my room and open my laptop, staring at the article I fell asleep reading last night.

The one that proves Tennessee wasn't lying after all.

CHAPTER NINE

LESSA

BEFORE

When he gets home from work that day, I've covered the bed with various shopping bags and I'm sitting in the middle of them, sorting through my purchases.

"What's all this?" He eyes me, kicking off his boots and placing them in his closet.

I hold up a sheer curtain. "I'm redecorating. What do you think of this?"

"Redecorating?" He balks. "What do you mean?"

"This place could use some sprucing up." I shrug one shoulder. "I ordered a new couch too, so we'll have to decide what to do about the old one."

He sinks onto the end of the bed, running a hand through his hair as he narrows his eyes at me.

"What?" I tilt my head to the side, a small smile on my lips.

"You didn't think you should run all of this by me first?"

His tone is harsher than I expected, and my smile slips away immediately. He almost sounds...*angry*. But why?

"I...I thought you'd like it. I thought it would be a nice surprise. You're always complaining about your old furniture, and you don't have any curtains at all—just blinds!"

"Always complaining?" He shakes his head, standing up again. "Always? I might've mentioned it once." He jabs a finger into the air. "*Once*. That my couch was starting to show its age. For God's sake, Lessa, I wasn't asking you to go out and buy me a new one."

"I thought I was doing something nice..." I drop the curtain with a huff. "Why are you so mad at me?"

"Because I like my stuff the way it is!" he shouts, then lowers his voice again, a hand up in surrender. I get the sense he's trying to control his temper. "Look, I'm not mad, okay? I'm just... I like my stuff. I like my stuff the way it is, and I can buy my own when I need it. I don't need you to buy me things. I don't need you to redecorate my place."

"Your place?" His words slam into me. "*Yours?* Not ours?"

"You're supposed to be getting your own place, remember?" He tugs one of the curtains from the bed, running it through his fingers with obvious disappointment, and tosses it back down. "You don't live here, Lessa."

"Really?" I jerk open the drawer of the nightstand, grabbing a handful of my camisoles. "Could've fooled me. Most of my stuff is here, Paul. I've been staying here every day for the past few months. How can you say I don't live here?"

"Look..." He sinks down on the edge of the bed, easing the drawer closed before he takes my hands in his. "It's not that I don't want you to stay with me. I love having you here.

It's just that..." His gaze travels the room with a look of obvious disdain. "You don't belong here. Not in this place—"

"That's why I'm trying to fix it up—"

"Yeah, but I don't want that. I like my place. I've worked hard for it. This is where I belong. Not in a place with"—he picks up one of the curtains from a bag on his left with two fingers, as if it's contaminated—"lacy, frilly little window things. Or with new couches. I want to be able to drink beer on my furniture at the end of a long day and not worry about whether I spill something on it."

"If you spill something on it, we'll just get a new one."

He sighs, dropping his head. "That's not what I'm... You're just not getting it—"

I hold his hands between mine. "So help me. Help me understand."

"I want to give you everything, Lessa. Really, I do. I want to give you everything you're used to and so much more. But I don't know that I'll ever be able to do that. I want to get you out of this shitty apartment and buy you a home that you'll love. A home that you can fill with all this..." He trails off, waving a hand over the bags. "But right now, I just can't."

"But that's not what I want. I don't want you to worry about what you can give me. Don't you get that? I just want to be with you."

"Really?" He quirks a brow. "Cause it sure as shit looks like you're trying to put lipstick on a pig here."

I laugh. "I'm just trying to do something nice for you. I don't care about any of this." Gripping as many of the bags as I can, I toss them to the floor. "I'll send them all back, cancel the couch. I just want you." I press my finger into his chest. "Just you and me. The rest doesn't matter."

His lips meet mine cautiously. "Are you sure about this?" It's like he's been waiting to ask me the question our whole relationship. Like he's been scared of knowing the answer. "Are you sure I'm going to be enough for you?"

"Positively positive. You're *more* than enough," I whisper, kissing him back.

At least, for the moment, I mean every word.

CHAPTER TEN

BLAKELY

PRESENT DAY

I t's just after two when I hear the doorbell ring upstairs. I listen for footsteps, for a sign that anyone is coming, but I hear nothing.

My phone rings, and I glance down at it, momentarily forgetting the doorbell when I spy my best friend's name on the screen.

"Hello?"

"Hey..." She's hesitant and I know why, but I won't bring it up. I hope she won't either, though I know better. "You never called me back. How are things going?"

"I'm sorry. I've just been...busy writing. You know how I get. How are things back home?"

"Fine, I guess... So, you've actually been able to get some words in? That's amazing, Blakely."

I glance guiltily at the laptop resting on my legs. "Um, yeah, well, it's nothing groundbreaking, trust me. But I'm trying, at least." More than I've done in a long time, but still not enough.

She sucks in a breath. "I'm so happy for you. I know what a relief it must be. And we both know trying is all that matters. Are you... Are you doing okay?"

"I'm fine, Katy, I promise. How's my girl?"

As if on cue, I hear my goddaughter crying in the background.

"Growing like a weed." Her voice is soft.

"And how's Noah?"

"Perfect as always. Handsome as ever." His voice is muffled when he answers, and I hear Katy giggle just before she kisses him.

I shake my head. They're so annoyingly adorable it makes my heart swell. She deserves it, she really does, but that doesn't mean it doesn't hurt.

It all just hurts.

The doorbell rings upstairs again, reminding me someone's at the door, and I stand up from the bed, running a hand over my yoga pants to smooth the wrinkles. "Hey, I have to go."

"What? No. Please, I want to talk to you."

"Someone's at the door. I'll call you back."

"Are you just avoiding me? Look, I know how hard this is, but I don't like you being there alone right now. You should be back home. With people who love you. With us."

"I'm not alone." I close the laptop, pacing the room. "And I'm fine. I swear. I love you, but I'm fine. I'll call you back."

Without waiting for permission, which I'm sure won't come anyway, I end the call and toss my phone on the bed.

Lyra's bedroom door is closed as I make my way up the

stairs and onto the first floor. Just beyond the glass of the door, I spy the faint silhouette of an older woman, her face muddled by the opaque window.

What in the world?

I swing the door open and take in her appearance. She's small, both thin and short, with long, gray hair tied back in a loose ponytail at the nape of her neck. Her face is wrinkled and makeup-free, her bright-blue eyes shining back at me from behind silver brows. When she smiles, my eyes fall to her mouth. There's something oddly familiar about her.

"Hello. Can I help you?" I grip the door, listening carefully for the sounds of my roommates emerging from their spaces.

"Well, actually, I was hoping *I* could help *you*." Her eyes twinkle, her voice soft and strained. "Are you Lyra?"

"I'm..." The question catches me off guard, but then fills me with relief. She must be a friend. But then why wouldn't she know I'm clearly not Lyra? "Sorry, who did you say you were?"

"I'm Lucy." She holds out a hand, and I shake it slowly. Her hand is frail in mine—I can feel the bones of it beneath her thin skin. "The property manager. We received a message about a hot tub malfunctioning, but our phones have been on the fritz all week, so I thought I'd just come down and see what the problem is, rather than waiting for them to be fixed."

"Oh." It all comes together for me in an instant. "Right. I'm so sorry. Of course." I step back, allowing her inside the house. "Lyra's downstairs, but I can show you where the—er, actually, I guess you already know where it is, hmm?" I step back, allowing her to lead the way, which she does, heading straight for the sliding glass door.

As we walk, I can't help noticing the clutter. A stack of books lying on the kitchen table and there are dirty dishes in the sink. The floor has mud on it from someone's shoes— likely the ones that are blocking the doorway until I kick them out of the way. She opens the door and steps out onto the porch without a word, but I have to wonder if she thinks we're slobs. Should I apologize for the mess? Promise we'll clean up before we leave?

As she sets to work looking around the hot tub, I find myself thinking this is the last person I'd expect to see showing up for a maintenance request. Like my other racing thoughts, I keep that one to myself as Lucy dawdles around the hot tub. Should I leave her to it, or would that be rude? She pushes the top off, sticking her hand into the water and withdrawing it quickly.

"Goodness, me! We certainly do have a problem, don't we?" She shakes off her hand, swiping it across the leg of her black jeans before she opens a panel on the side, flipping one switch and then another. Her lips pinch together as she glances around. "Hmm..." She stands, face lit up as if she's just thought of something, and makes her way toward the house again. Leaning against the wall, she unplugs the tub, then plugs it in again.

Five minutes of her poking and prodding, plugging and unplugging later, and she finally sighs, hands pressed into her hips. "Well, I suppose whatever's going on, I'm not going to be able to fix it on my own. I'll have to put in a call to our maintenance team." She grins with a twinkle in her eyes. "You'll love them."

"Oh, okay." I try—and fail, I'd guess—to hide my disappointment. "Do you know when they'll be able to come?"

"Best guess is tomorrow, if we're lucky. Remind me, how much longer are you all here for?"

"We check out Saturday, so just three more nights after tonight."

She nods. "Hmm. Well, I'll see what we can do. I'm really sorry. I can't imagine what could've happened." She tugs the cover back onto the hot tub. "I know it was working fine when the cleaners came in over the weekend."

Something about her tone feels accusatory. Does she think we broke it?

"It was working fine last night, too. But when we woke up, it had just stopped. We followed all of the instructions. It's like it just went out or something."

"Well, we'll get it all situated, don't you worry." She pats my arm, and I regret my sharp tone instantly. "Let me write down my number for you, too. That way if you can't get a hold of the office, you can just call me. Actually, you'd better just call me anyway, in case the phones are still down."

"Okay. Thank you, Lucy."

Back inside, she digs through one of the drawers with a familiarity that puts me at ease. Maybe until that moment, I wasn't one-hundred-percent certain she was who she said she was.

She scribbles her number on a scrap piece of paper and slides it across the table to me. "There you go. Just give me a call if you need anything else. I'll have you fixed up in a jiffy."

"Thanks, Lucy." I tap the paper.

"Of course. Now, I should get back to the office before

the girls miss me too much. I'll call the maintenance line as soon as I get in the car."

I walk her out and head back down to my room, my mind already on the chapter I've been neglecting, and the article that has become my obsession.

By the evening, I've nearly forgotten about Lucy, and hardly notice when the maintenance team doesn't arrive at all.

CHAPTER ELEVEN

LESSA

BEFORE

The door opens and then slams shut moments later. The sound of his heavy footsteps making his way across the apartment hardly registers.

A few moments later, his tool bag hits the ground.

"Why aren't you ready?"

I hear the words but can't bring myself to respond. My mouth is dry, my head fuzzy. He walks around the couch, standing in front of where I'm sitting, my legs pulled up underneath me and my hands lost in the depths of my over-sized sweatshirt.

I blink.

Once.

Twice.

Then, I look up at him.

"Whoa... Hey... What's wrong?" He drops down in front of me, hands on my knees. "What happened?"

Is it the tears he sees? Or the panic?

"I..." I open my mouth, but no words form. No thoughts form. There's just...nothing. A system malfunction.

"Are you sick? Are you hurt?" He's looking me over with terror in his eyes, and I want to calm him, to tell him everything's okay, but it would be a lie.

I shake my head as his eyes and hands trail my body, looking for a sign as to why I'm still sitting here when I should be dressed and ready for our anniversary dinner. I drop my head, chin to my chest, and release a heavy sob.

He wraps me in his arms, moving to sit on the couch as he rocks us back and forth. "Oh, baby... It's going to be okay." He has no idea what he's even talking about. No idea what's coming next.

I shake my head against his shoulder as his thumb comes up to dry my tears. "It's going to be okay," he repeats. "Whatever it is, I'm here. It'll all be okay."

"I don't think it is." My voice is soft, so soft I'm not sure I actually said the words aloud.

"What's going on? Talk to me, Lessa. You're scaring me." He pulls away from me, looking into my eyes with trepidation.

"I..."

"You what? Did something happen? Is it your parents?"

He wishes.

Maybe I do, too. It would certainly make this next part easier.

"No. I, um..." My hand comes to rest on my stomach as I sniffle, and he registers the movement, his cheeks paling. He gives a half shake of his head—as if to ward off what I'm going to say—just as I begin to speak. "I'm pregnant."

His hands drop away from me. "What?" The horror on his face is painful. This wasn't in the plans. We've been so careful. So painstakingly careful.

"I'm pregnant, Paul." I swipe under my nose with the back of my hand. "*We're* pregnant."

"H-how... How is that possible?" He backs away, eyes wide.

"I really don't know, but I took three tests. All positive."

He nods, but his gaze is lost. He's not looking at me, not looking at anything, really. It's the same state he found me in only moments ago.

He sinks back into the couch, and there we sit, shoulder to shoulder, the weight of the world ready to crush us.

After what feels like an eternity, he huffs out a breath and asks the single question that's been haunting me since the moment I saw the first set of two pink lines.

"What do you want to do?"

I close my eyes. Today was supposed to be a happy day. Our first anniversary. We were supposed to get dressed up, have a nice weekend away, lots of wine, even more sex.

But now...the idea of moving off this couch feels too ambitious.

"I have no idea."

"Okay..." His hand moves to grip my knee, assuring me that, in this moment and all others, we're still in this together.

"We should get married," I whisper, after a moment's pause. "If we don't, my parents will force me to move back home. They'll force us to break up. It's the only way..."

The only way, what? I'm not sure. What I do know is that it's the only thing that makes sense in my head. I'm not sure we're ready—I'm not sure I even want to do it—but if we're going to have this baby, it's the only logical path forward.

"My parents will use every tool at their disposal to bring me home. To tear us apart. But if we're married—"

"Okay." He cuts me off, turning to stare at me. "Okay."

I can't read his expression. Is it love or happiness or fear? All I know is that he smiles at me and, for the first time all day, I think maybe he's right. Maybe things will actually be okay.

CHAPTER TWELVE

BLAKELY

PRESENT DAY

I wake earlier than everyone else the next morning. The weight of the anniversary hits me with my first breath, before the consciousness has even set in. I take two pain pills, hoping to dull the ache, though it's coming from my heart today, rather than my head like usual.

The pain today is just as real as it was that day.

If I don't keep moving, I'll never make it through.

So, like many days over the past year, I push myself up from the bed, forcing the thoughts from my mind, and slip into the bathroom.

After doing the bare minimum to make myself presentable, I step into my shoes and head for the door.

Outside, the fresh mountain air is intoxicating—both somehow a comfort and a painful reminder of everything that has happened.

A reminder that I am, and will always be, alone.

The woods are quiet around me, except for the occasional hoot of an owl or call of a bird. I wrap my arms tighter around myself, trying to warm the bitter chill that rests somewhere deep inside my bones, the place that never seems to warm.

A twig snaps behind me, and I spin around, whipping my gaze from this side to that. "Hello?"

The only response is the sound of the wind through the trees.

Probably just an animal.

With my attention turned back to the path ahead, I take another step and freeze when I hear it again. Somewhere behind me, someone is following.

This time, I don't dare turn around and give away what I've realized. Instead, I move forward, one step, then another...

Three more quick steps.

Then, I slip behind a tree and wait.

I listen.

They're moving again...

Someone is coming behind me. They're cautious. They believe their steps are silent, but they're wrong. I hear them. I know they're approaching, and I'm prepared. I reach down slowly, taking hold of a branch on the ground.

I lift it and clutch it to my chest.

As the footsteps grow nearer, I grip the branch tighter, my only defense against whomever or whatever is coming for me.

The footsteps have stopped, and my heart thuds in my ears. Are they gone? Have they lost me? Or are they simply waiting for me to appear? Waiting for me to stick my head out from behind this tree so they can catch me?

So they can...kill me?

Oh my God, I'm being so dramatic, even to my own... ears? Mind? I don't know. I wish Tennessee would've never brought up what happened here. I've let him get in my head, and I'm driving myself crazy stressing over it.

Still, when I hear another footstep, I suck in a sharp, ragged breath, squeezing my lips together to silence it as I decide my next move.

Where are they?

Who are they?

The silence that follows is deafening.

"*Boo.*"

I jump, swinging the stick with all my might as an amused Tennessee jumps back from my side, narrowly missing getting a branch to the temple.

"Jesus!" he shouts, swatting the branch away. "Take out an eye, why don't ya?"

"What *is* your problem?" I demand, shoving my hands down at my sides. A rage-induced headache pounds in my temples. "Why are you doing this?"

"Doing what?" The smirk fades a smidge. *Just* a smidge.

"Trying to scare us so much."

"What? I'm not." His innocent act is convincing.

"Tennessee, *why* are you following me?"

He tries to pull the branch from my hands, but I refuse to release it, and eventually, he relents, both palms on display. "Look, I'm sorry. I wasn't following you. I didn't mean to scare you. I was out for a walk and I saw you. You looked upset. I wanted to make sure everything was okay."

"So you snuck up behind me and said *boo?*" He blinks, seeming to reconsider his actions, but I don't give him a chance to apologize—if he was even planning to. "I'm fine, Tennessee. I don't need you to look after me."

"Point taken." He backs up half a step. "I'm sorry. I saw you walking alone in the woods and was worried about you."

"Why?"

He scoffs. "*Why?*"

"Yes. Why? You don't know me."

"Well, *A*, I kind of feel like I do, and *B*, I don't have to know you to want you to stay safe. Whoever you are, you're a woman alone in the woods. I didn't want anyone to...I don't know...bother you, or something."

"Well, funny thing is, the only person *bothering* me is you."

I don't know why I'm being so rude to him.

No, actually, I do know.

"If you want me to leave you alone, I will. I was just trying to be a gentleman."

"No, I think you just like to scare me. Scare us."

His brows draw down. "I wasn't trying to scare you, Blakely. I didn't even know you knew I was there. Honestly, I was trying to keep back and make sure you were safe. Then, when I found you, I..." He runs a hand through his hair with a sigh. "I don't know why I said *boo*, honestly. It was a joke, and obviously in poor taste. If I scared you, I swear that wasn't my intention."

I shake my head. "I never said you scared me."

He glances at the branch in my hands. "Clearly."

I drop it, my hands locked at my sides, and spin around to head in the direction of the house.

"You don't have to leave on my account. I'll go back inside."

"No, I should get back to work anyway."

His hand comes down on my shoulder. "Will you just wait a second?"

I spin away, jerking out of his grasp. "Wait for *what?*"

"Look, I think we got off on the wrong foot. I'm sorry for whatever I've done to piss you off, but I'd like to think we can be civil. We're all stuck in this house for the rest of the week, so the least we can do is get along. Why are you so mad at me, anyway?"

"I'm not mad at you. I don't like you. There's a difference."

He's unfazed, which only makes me angrier. "Okay, so then, why don't you like me?"

"Because I don't."

He crosses his arms, but I don't budge. I don't owe him the truth. Don't owe anyone the truth.

"I don't believe that. There's something more going on. Will you please tell me?"

"Why do you even care, Tennessee?" I sigh.

"I feel like we've already been over that. I care because it's the decent thing to do."

"And who said you were decent?"

The comment stings. I see it written on his face, but you'd never know it from his next words. "I don't know. I like to think I am."

I purse my lips, fighting against another mean comment, ready to hurl the next insult at him. He doesn't deserve it. This has nothing to do with him. I know that, somewhere deep in the rational part of my brain. But today is not a day for rationality.

"Look, if it's about the other night... I was joking. Obviously I was joking. I'll tell everyone I was lying if that will make you feel better. I'd had a few drinks, and I was just... saying stupid stuff. I made it all up."

"You did not. Don't bother lying now." I swallow, studying him.

"What?"

"I know you weren't lying. I looked it up. Everything you said happened here—the man who died—it's true."

"Oh, right. The internet is a thing that exists." He rolls his eyes, looking away. "Fine, so, I wasn't lying—"

"Why would you try to say that you were?"

"Jesus." He releases a heavy breath. "What do you want from me, Blakely? Look, I'm just trying to say or do the right thing here. What do you want me to say?"

"I'm fine, okay, Tennessee? I'm fine. We're fine. Can we just move on from all of this?"

He reaches for me again as I move away, but I'm faster. Barely, but still faster. "Why don't I believe you?"

"Can you just—" A sob threatens to escape from my throat, and I bite back the rest of my sentence. "Please. Please just leave me alone."

"*Wait...* What's wrong?"

"Look, I just need to go." This time, when he tries to stop me, I'm faster. I'm feet away when I hear him speak again.

"For the record, this all felt wrong to me."

Something in his voice stops me in my tracks. "What?"

"When I got the email with the invitation for this weekend, I almost turned it down."

I spin back around to face him, sensing the truth in his words. "Why?"

"Because of what happened here. Despite what you may believe, I'm not a heartless monster. Growing up, I didn't remember the actual murder that happened. I mean, I knew about it, but I wasn't old enough to understand any of it, so it was never really sad or anything for me. I don't mean for that to sound bad, it's just something I was kind of separated from. But it started feeling scary as I got older. I remember there were all these rumors about kids who would come out here and try to stay the night, or try to come in without a flashlight, whatever, and they'd hear babies crying or footsteps or screams. My mom always warned me to stay away from here. She didn't believe it was haunted, as far as I could tell, but I think people tended to take advantage of it being empty in order for them to do all sorts of shady stuff. Drugs, mostly. Anyway, then a year or so ago, I heard someone had bought it and was redoing it. Some sort of investor. They were turning it into a writer's retreat because of the history."

He chews his bottom lip thoughtfully, perhaps waiting for me to say something, but I can't. I'm terrified of what will come out if I open my mouth.

"Anyway, so when I got the email, it felt wrong. Like they were trying to profit off someone else's tragedy. But I was also curious. I wanted to see it for myself. See what they'd done to it."

"Do you know what happened here?"

"I know what I've read online—same as you, I'm guessing. The stories that went around town were always wildly different, but from what I can tell, they think it might've been a kidnapping. The husband was found dead by the police when his employer reported he hadn't shown up for work for a few weeks. The wife and son were never found, but most people think they're dead by now. And, if she's not dead, everyone else believes she either fell in love and ran off with someone else or she's guilty herself."

I swallow.

"Is that what you read, too?"

"Basically, yeah. I didn't read very much. Just enough to convince me you weren't lying."

"I wish I was."

"Me too."

His smile is soft. "It was terrible, but it's in the past. We've been here all this time and, I have to say, I've never once heard nor seen a ghost." The attempted joke falls flat, and I look down as a tear cascades down my cheek.

"I should go back inside."

Before he can object, I'm gone.

CHAPTER THIRTEEN

LESSA

BEFORE

The wedding is small, the guest list smaller. It's nothing like I dreamed of as a little girl. *Do most people feel this way?* I wonder. *Does it always feel like it will be bigger, better, brighter in your mind, somehow?* I've found so many things in life to be letdowns, and I have to wonder if that means there's something wrong with me, or if everyone else is just pretending to be so happy and in awe of life.

Still, I put on my dress, thankful the fabric has yet to feel tight against my abdomen.

The baby's the size of a lemon now, according to my doctor. I can't feel him or her yet. If it weren't for the morning sickness, I might not know anything had changed. But it has. Everything has changed. Me, standing here in a white dress, preparing to walk down the aisle at any moment is proof of that.

Paul and I were supposed to be having fun.

We were supposed to enjoy our time getting to know each other.

I don't resent our child—I should probably get that out of the way. But I'm not as happy about it as I should be. Does that make sense?

It's scary, really. To know I'm going to be a mother when I still feel so much like a child.

To know someone is going to be depending on me to keep them alive.

I invited my parents to the wedding, but they have no idea about the baby yet. I can't tell them. I don't know why I can't. Paul keeps telling me how silly it is, how I'm a grown woman, and asking what are they going to do, ground me?

Excellent question.

One I don't have an answer to.

I *am* a grown woman. I know that.

But my parents are all-powerful. They control this town and everyone in it, so what's there to stop them from controlling me?

This feels like the only way out of their grasp, but sometimes I feel like I'm trading one prison for another.

I love Paul, I really do, but this isn't what I thought my life would look like. I'm not even sure I want to get married or have kids, and yet, here I am, walking down the aisle as if led by some other force.

As if my life isn't even mine anymore.

I check the small window in the back of the room, staring out into the parking lot. This is the moment I could run, if I wanted to.

But run where? And to whom?

My parents would find me. I'd break Paul's heart.

The fact of the matter is, in a world full of options, I currently have none.

And so, as the music starts, interrupting my thoughts, I walk through the door and toward the aisle. My dad isn't there waiting. He's not going to walk me down the aisle— says he has no desire to give me to Paul and won't lie in church about doing so.

The preacher will leave out that part. Won't ask who's giving me to Paul. Won't ask for their blessing.

He'll move right along just as I do now, down the aisle, with Paul standing up ahead, looking just as terrified as I am.

Maybe that's why everything went so wrong. Maybe we were doomed from the start.

CHAPTER FOURTEEN

BLAKELY

PRESENT DAY

I should be writing, but instead, I'm reading over the article for what feels like the hundredth time just today. Tennessee got it almost completely right—a husband slaughtered in the kitchen; a young son and the mother missing; no suspects ever named.

What he left out—either because he doesn't know or because he doesn't think it's relevant—is that the woman was incredibly wealthy. Her family had made their money in oil and various business ventures, and she was set to inherit it all until she disappeared. Like Tennessee mentioned, people speculated it might've been a kidnapping-for-ransom situation, but as far as I can tell, no such demands ever came.

The family pictures are particularly painful, and they litter the internet. Though not immediately.

No, the new owners have made sure of that, I bet. When you search for the address, you simply find the website for the newly founded writer's retreat—gorgeous, flattering pictures of every inch of the home. But, once you know the family name—Lessa and Paul Brody—the search results change instantly.

It happened less than thirty years ago. My blood goes cold when I think about that, so I try not to.

So much pain in this house.

Within these walls.

Pain.

It's something I know well.

I force the thought away and close out of the article. I need to work. This book isn't going to write itself, and I don't have much more time.

The retreat ends in just a few days, and what will I have to show for it?

I open the blank document, the blinking cursor taunting me. I type a sentence, then erase it, and repeat the process several times.

An hour later, I have two paragraphs written.

Two terrible paragraphs.

It's not much, but it's something, I guess. At this point, I'll take anything I can get.

In the hallway, a door slams and I look up, my body suddenly tense. Seconds later, footsteps pound up the staircase.

I turn my attention back to my laptop.

Come on.

Focus.

Just finish the chapter.

Just as I'm starting to write again, the footsteps are back. This time, they're descending the stairs. I glance at the doorway seconds before someone knocks. Sliding the laptop from my legs, I stand and swing the door open.

Lyra is there, her lips pressed into a thin smile.

"Everything okay?"

"I'm looking for my phone."

"Your *phone?*"

"Yes, my phone. An iPhone in a white case. Have you seen it?"

"I'm sorry... No. Why would I? I've been down here most of the morning. Where did you last—"

She scoffs. "Of course you haven't."

"Did you expect me to? Is it missing or something?"

Her eyes cut to me, her lips forming a grimace. "Yeah, missing *or something.* I can't find it anywhere. Just like my notes on Monday." She pushes away from my door, turning to walk back to her room with a groan.

"Would you like me to help you look for it?" I'm no longer as patient as I was a few days ago. She's pissing me off at this point, and I'm not going to hide it.

"Can someone call it, please?" She yells this up the stairs, obviously not directing the request at me.

"On it." That's Aidy. A few seconds later, she says, "It's ringing."

I want to ask how she has Lyra's phone number... I haven't exchanged with anyone since we arrived. Did they leave me out of that on purpose?

I shove down my anxiety and focus on the task at hand. Or, at least, I try to anyway.

"I don't hear anything," Lyra says with a groan.

"Where did you have it last?" I repeat the question I tried to ask before.

"It's been on my nightstand all morning. I went upstairs to get something to eat and stepped outside for a minute, and when I came back to my room, it was gone." She's not really talking to me—more like talking over me—as her eyes search the hallway and the downstairs living room.

"I didn't take it," I say. "And I haven't heard anyone down here."

"Well, obviously *someone* was down here, because my phone was here and now it isn't." She pushes open her bedroom door and steps inside, moving to search around the nightstand. Unsure of what to do, I join her in the room. I'm cautious at first, but as soon as I'm sure she's not going to send me away, I drop to the floor to look under the bed, in case it's fallen there.

A random sock is all that awaits me. I sit up on my knees. "Did you take it into the bathroom with you, by any chance? Or...could it be in your pocket?" I stand up and check the sliding glass door to her private patio, making sure it's locked, and it is.

She shoves her hands in both pockets, obviously more worried than annoyed at this point, and shakes her head. When she looks at me, I see panic shining back. "Where could it have gone, Blakely? It was right here. I'm positive. It's like it just...disappeared."

CHAPTER FIFTEEN

LESSA

BEFORE

I'm a wife.

A wife.

Paul's wife.

No matter how many times I repeat those words in my head, they still don't seem completely real. The nerves I felt on my wedding day are gone, though, replaced by overwhelming happiness. I don't know why I was so worried, to be honest. My husband is an amazing person. He's a man I've wanted to meet my whole life.

Someone from outside of my world. Someone who will love me for who I am, not what I can offer him.

Now, I wear his last name like a badge of honor, and the tiny diamond wedding band like a crown. It's not much, but it's everything just the same.

I'm growing now and halfway through the pregnancy. Soon, we'll find out what we're having. I keep thinking it's a boy, though I have nothing other than a mother's intuition to explain the theory. Either way, we haven't decided on a name yet. I'm so big at this point, I keep forgetting to account for my new size and bump into countertops often.

I run a hand over my stomach when I feel the baby kick, as if he knows I'm thinking about him.

I'm still scared, don't get me wrong, but I love this baby more than I thought I could. For now, that's enough.

When the door opens, I check the clock on the newly painted wall. There are still at least three hours before Paul should be home, but no one else has a key. I grab the first thing I see—a coffee mug—to use as a weapon and raise it above my head as the footsteps grow closer. I move around the end of the new sofa, pinning it between me and the doorway.

When Paul enters, I drop the mug to my side with a breath of relief, but when I see his face, the relief washes away like sand near the ocean.

"What happened?" I swallow.

He shakes his head, running a hand over his dirt-caked cheeks. "The project's shut down."

"Shut down? For...for how long?"

"For a long-ass time, the way they talked. Maybe permanently."

"So what does that mean for you?"

"It means I'm out of work." He kicks off his boots. "Caleb isn't sure when there will be more."

"I don't understand. Why can't he just put you on a new project?"

"Because everything's already contracted out right now. He's looking for new projects to bid on, but..." He shakes his head. "The Astors own half the contracting companies in town, and they can beat everyone's bids because they pay their people next to nothing."

He says my parents' name rather than calling them my parents in order to separate me from them, but it does little to help. They're still my parents, and now it sounds like they'll be my downfall. Maybe this is what they wanted all along.

"Caleb will figure out something, though, right? I mean, we'll be okay." My hand falls to my belly again. "He'll find you work again."

"Eventually, yeah, but...I don't know." He moves toward the hallway, shoulders slumped.

"So what does that mean? Are we okay? Will we... Do we need help? How can this just happen?"

He spins on his heel. "Welcome to the real world, Lessa. Where nothing is guaranteed. There are no cushions to fall back on, no nest egg. For most of us, everything can change from one second to the next. And, apparently, this is our second."

I grind my teeth together, staring at him. Why is he being so mean to me? It's not like *I* did this. It's not like I have any say in any of this. "What are you saying?"

"I'm saying things are about to get really complicated, okay? We have enough money in the account to last us the month, maybe. With my final paycheck, I think we'll be okay, but if I can't find a job..." He shrugs. "I don't know. If I can't find something soon, we'll lose the apartment. And my car too, probably. Which means we may have to sell yours."

I shake my head. There's no way I'm selling my convertible. It was a present for my sixteenth birthday, and it's been with me through everything. It's out of the question, but I can't tell him that. He'll call me ridiculous or childish.

"I could ask my parents for help." My parents stopped sending money after the wedding, but I don't believe they'd rather have me starving or homeless than help us out. I've seen them spend our entire month's expenses on dinner before. It would be nothing to them.

"Or you could get a job yourself."

I narrow my gaze at him. He's just angry—I know that. I try to remind myself of it, but that doesn't make it sting any less. "You know I'm trying to write a book."

He scoffs and turns away. "Yeah, I know. *This* week."

"What's that supposed to mean?"

"It means you change your mind like you change your socks, and get wild hairs up your ass about random business ventures you never see through. Last month, you were going to start a makeup brand. Six months ago, you wanted to open a salon. We don't have the kind of luxury you're used to anymore. I've been carrying us on my own, but I can't do that right now, Lessa. It's not realistic for you to spend your days writing a book that might never sell when we're literally about to lose our apartment. Don't you get th—"

"It can't sell if it's not written! You've never acted like you were bothered by my random ideas before. I'm just trying to figure out what I'm passion—"

"Yeah, while I was employed, sure, I wasn't bothered. Not really, anyway. But we have responsibilities now. A baby. Rent. A car. My job covered us, but right now, we can't both be unemployed." He sighs, shoving his hands into his pockets. "Look. It's not a big deal, okay? Plenty of women work. And plenty of writers have day jobs. It's all part of it."

"Well, it's not part of it for me." I cross my arms over my chest. "I'm allowed to do what I'm passionate about. It's my birthright."

"Birthright." He rolls his eyes. "You're not a goddamn princess, Lessa. I'm not saying you can't do what you love. But would you rather get a day job—at least temporarily until I can find work—or lose everything? Because those are our options as they currently stand."

"I'd rather call my parents."

He presses his lips together with obvious frustration, puffing out a breath. "Mommy and Daddy can't always save you. That's not real life."

"That's *my* real life."

"Not anymore." He steps forward, anger radiating off him, and suddenly, we're nose to nose. "I'll be damned if your parents, who seem hell-bent on ruining our lives, have any say in getting us out of this mess. I'll figure it out. I'll take care of you."

"How are *you* taking care of me by forcing *me* to go to work?"

"*Forcing* you? Jesus Christ, what sort of alternate reality are you living in?" He steps back, running a hand through his hair. "I should've known this was how it would go. Should've known you could never just be normal."

"Meaning what?"

"Meaning we're too different. We aren't just from two different sides of town. We're from two different *worlds*. I thought I could overlook that, but I can't."

"So, you're...what? You're...you're leaving me?"

"No. I don't know. I just need some time, okay?" He

steps around me, heading back toward the door. When I reach for his arm, he shrugs me off.

"Paul, wait! Please."

The door slams shut moments later, and I'm left with only his tool bag and a million questions.

I walk into the kitchen and pick up the phone, dialing my parents' number.

Indira answers. "Astor residence."

"Indira, it's me. Can I speak to my dad please?"

"One moment."

She places the phone down and, a few minutes later, my dad's voice fills the line. "Sweetheart, what is it? What's wrong?"

"Daddy, I... I need help."

"Where are you? Do you want me to send a car for you?"

"No." I stifle a sob.

"What's going on?" I hear my mother's voice in the background.

"Paul got laid off today. The project they were working on downtown was postponed or something... I don't know what to do."

"You come home," he says firmly. "That's what you do. You come home, and your mother and I will help you. We'll get you through the divorce. We can build a nursery for the child. Just come home and everything will be okay."

"I can't leave him, Daddy..."

He sighs. "Can't you see he's doing nothing but bringing you down? Hurting you? You weren't meant to live this way, Lessa. We didn't raise you like this."

"It's not his fault. He's a good man."

"I'm not saying he's not. But he's not... Not *like us*. Not like you." He pauses, and I hear a heavy breath. "Come home, and we'll fix all of this."

"And if I don't? Then, you won't help me? Won't help your grandchild?"

"*Until*,"—he stresses the word—"you come home, we don't have a grandchild."

With that, the call ends.

CHAPTER SIXTEEN

BLAKELY

PRESENT DAY

"You had to have moved it somewhere," Daniel says, shaking his head from where he stands at the kitchen island. "Why would any of us have taken it?"

"Same reason someone took my notes." Lyra glares at him from across the room, her hands digging into her hips. She's really on a rampage at this point, accusing everyone in her path of having something to do with her missing phone.

"Which is?"

"To freak me out. To make me look crazy. Your guess is as good as mine."

Daniel looks down, returning his attention to the apple he's washing. Near him, Tennessee has his back resting against a countertop, the wrinkles in his forehead clearly pronounced. Aidy is sitting next to me on the couch, while Lyra moves around the open space of the living room, overturning this and that and looking in all the places we've already looked.

It doesn't make any sense. How could something just disappear?

I don't want to admit it, but part of me wonders if Lyra is doing this to scare us all, or upset us maybe. Same with her missing notes that were on her nightstand all along. Either that or someone clearly has something against her.

I can't figure out anything else that would explain why it seems to only be her things going missing or being misplaced.

"Look, the fact is, it's not in the house," Tennessee says after a moment. "We've looked all over, called it, tried to access it via Find My iPhone, and it's not here. So, you need to call your cell phone provider and report it as lost. At least for now. You can use my phone to do that, if you want."

She looks at each of us, maybe hoping we'll defend her or say he's wrong, but as far as I can see, he's not. Wherever her phone is, we can't find it. Maybe she left it out on the porch and it fell somewhere and she doesn't want to admit it. Maybe she dropped it in the toilet and doesn't want to tell us. All I know is that I've lost an hour of my life looking for this phone, and I need to get back to work.

"I need to run to town," she says after a moment. "But I can't call an Uber without my phone."

"I can drive you," Aidy offers, her voice quiet, almost as if she wishes she hadn't spoken. "I rented a car for the week."

Lyra gives her a small smile. "Thank you. I would appreciate that. Just let me go change clothes."

Aidy follows suit, heading to her own room as well, and returning a few moments later, freshly changed into a white T-shirt with a cat's face on it and black, loose-fitting pants covered in pumpkins. Her dark hair is pulled back in a messy bun. When Lyra reappears, her pink business suit a stark contrast to Aidy's casual outfit, the two head out the door, leaving Daniel, Tennessee, and me alone.

"So, who's messing with her stuff?" Daniel eyes us both when the door closes.

The question catches me off guard, and I can tell by Tennessee's expression, he feels the same way.

Daniel laughs to himself. "Put a group of thriller writers together, I guess something's bound to happen."

"Yeah, I guess." Tennessee's words are apprehensive as he sinks into a chair at the dining room table across from us. "Hey, I've gotta ask, why are you here anyway? I mean...with us?"

Now it's Daniel who seems caught off guard as he moves across the room and sinks into an armchair. "Same reason the rest of you are, I guess. I could use the getaway to clear my head and the invitation came at just the right time."

"But why *this* group?" Tennessee presses. "Why did they choose us? It's not like we all move in the same circles. We're different subgenres, different places in our careers. I know they said we're some of their favorite authors, but I keep going over and over it in my head. I guess I'm asking... Do you think each of us was chosen for a reason beyond that?"

Daniel bites into his apple, chewing thoughtfully. His eyes fall to me as he chews, the wrinkles surrounding his eyes deepening. Finally, he looks back at Tennessee. "You're suggesting you think it's more than a coincidence?"

"If there's one thing I know, it's that there's no such thing as coincidence."

Daniel smiles with a closed mouth, then stands. As he moves past where Tennessee has sat down, he pats his shoulder. "I think you've written one too many crime novels, my friend."

We watch him climb the staircase without another word and, once his bedroom door shuts, Tennessee looks at me. "What about you? Do you believe this is all a coincidence?"

"I guess I hadn't really thought about it. I mean, what's the alternative?"

He stares at me, obviously weighing something, then nods, leaning forward over his legs. "What if this is all some sort of setup?"

I almost laugh. It's too much, really. "Setup? What are you talking about?"

"What if somehow Lyra brought us here to...to..."

"To what, Tennessee? To frame us for stealing her phone? This all seems pretty elaborate. And, besides, why would she even want to do that? Have we all wronged her somehow?" I tease. "Is this an elaborate ruse to make us pay for our sins?"

He drops back in his seat, running a hand over his face. "I have no idea. You're right, it's ridiculous. I think this place is starting to get to me." With a turn of his head, he stares out the window at the woods surrounding us.

Oddly, I know what he means. It's lonely up here with no one around. It's easy to forget the rest of the world exists. That we all have families and lives to return to after this.

The sky is painted brilliant shades of pink and orange as the sun sets into the horizon, reminding me that another day has come and gone. Reminding me I'm no closer to finishing this book than when I arrived three days ago.

"I should probably cook us something for dinner," I say, moving to stand. "I'm starving and losing track, but I think it's my turn to cook." In truth, I'm not sure we're taking turns at this point, as lately, we've all just been sort of fending for ourselves. But for now, I need something to keep my hands busy. Once, I loved cooking meals, but I haven't done it in a very long time.

I move to the kitchen and open the fridge, searching through the various dinner options. "How does vegetable soup sound?" Without waiting for an answer, I pull open the crisper drawer and grab several stalks of celery, carrots, spinach, and peppers. It's a recipe my mother used to make, and thinking of it has me both overwhelmed with missing her and desperate to make it to feel close to her. Grief is strange.

"Can I help?" Tennessee startles me by appearing at the edge of the counter when I turn around.

"Um, sure." I hand him the carrots before turning to the pantry to search for potatoes and onions. "Wash and dice them, please."

I half expect him to ask me how, but I am surprised when he pushes the sleeves of his shirt up and sets to work. We work side by side in silence, except for the rhythmic *chop, chop, chop* as we dice the vegetables.

Several minutes pass before I ask, "Do you like to cook?"

He laughs dryly. "I don't like to cook, necessarily, but I like to eat. My mom has always been really into healthy living—organic food, no dyes, no perfumes—"

"She was ahead of her time," I muse, hardly aware I've said it.

"Yeah, I guess you could say that." He lays down the

knife once he's finished with the carrots and grabs the onion, peeling back its outer layers. "Anyway, once I was out on my own, I preferred to cook my own meals because it's how I've always eaten. I'm not saying I cook everything from scratch, but...I don't know. There's something special about making something with your hands, you know?"

He catches me staring at him in what can only be described as wonder, and I look away. "I've always loved to cook, too. It was something I did with my mother growing up." I offer him a small smile, but can't bring myself to say more.

"That's all we're trying to do as writers, isn't it?"

"Hmm?"

"I mean, creating something with our hands. That's all we're doing, really. Creating entire worlds with our hands."

"I've never thought about it like that." In a way, he's not wrong. Writing is considered mentally draining, but what about the toll it takes on our bodies? Our backs and wrists and eyes? We're creating worlds not only with our minds, but with our hands and bodies too.

"I don't know. It's probably stupid." He waves away the thought.

"I don't think it's stupid at all." I place my knife down and rinse my hands, drying them on a towel before searching for a pot in one of the cabinets. "I think, actually, you're right."

He doesn't respond straight away. Then, he says, "Do you still cook with your mother?"

I shake my head from where I am, not turning to see if he's looking. "No. She...she died a few years ago."

"I lost my dad too."

"I'm so sorry."

"Me too." His voice is full of understanding. "Did she get to read any of your books?"

"A few, yes." I drop my head as the weight of the pain sends a shiver through me. *Not many. Not enough.* I don't say those words aloud, knowing how selfish they'll sound. "Did your dad?"

"No." He clears his throat, speaking a bit louder. "He died when I was just a kid. I think I still wanted to be an astronaut last time we talked." His laugh is bitter.

I place the pot on the stove and turn the cooktop on. "Your mom must be proud of you, though."

"She is." He nods and turns to me with a wink. "Shows me off to all her friends."

"I can see why." I press my lips together. "Your books are good."

He blanches, his jaw going slack. "You mean you've read them?"

"I've read two of them. One because a friend recommended them, and the other because we were on a panel together last year and I wanted to have something to talk to you about."

"Did we talk?" He scans his memory.

"No. We didn't." I shake my head. "It was busy after, and we didn't get a chance. Anyway, it wasn't a huge deal. But they were...they were good."

"I'm sorry I haven't read yours yet." His tone is genuine, and it almost makes me regret bringing it up, though I'm glad we're out of the awkward territory of talking about our dead parents.

"It's okay. I'm not really sure they'd be your kind of

thing." I busy myself with pouring broth into the pot before I begin to add the vegetables. "Will you bring those over here?"

"Yep." He passes by me on the way to the stove with a cutting board full of carrots. "I'll read them and let you know. But I'm sure they're great."

"I didn't say they weren't great," I tease. "Just that you might not like them."

"Oh, so you're insulting my taste now?"

"Well, there are no car chases, shoot-outs, or women with heaving bosoms staring longingly at themselves in the mirror, so...you tell me."

"Hey, I have never written about anyone's *bosom heaving*." He scowls. "I, at least, know better than that. I've seen the posts and articles that make fun of how men write women. Same as you."

I give an exaggerated frown. "Fine. I don't remember any of that in your books, you're right, but still...there are no car chases or heists. My stories are more subtle."

"Like you, you mean?"

I cast a glance at him and find him staring at me, seconds before he returns to chopping the onion. "Am I subtle?"

"You are."

"What makes you say that?"

"You're hard to read, Blakely. Hard to get a feel for."

"Are you trying to read me, Tennessee?" I smirked. "What on earth would you do that for?"

"Maybe I find you interesting."

"Well...I'm not that interesting, honestly. My books are the most interesting part of my life. Outside of that, I'm basically a reclusive cat lady."

"So you have cats?"

"*A* cat."

"See, I'm learning something new already."

"Do you have any pets?" We drop the last of the vegetables into the pot and I place the lid over the top. The glass immediately fogs.

"No. None. I travel too much to keep a pet alive."

I nod. "Makes sense. You're an extrovert, obviously."

"Obviously. I like to travel. Meet new people. And... since you're a self-proclaimed recluse, I'm going to assume you're not."

I hold up a hand. "Very much an introvert."

"Nothing wrong with that." He shakes his head. "I know we all talked a little bit about our families when we first got here, but remind me. Do you...live alone with this cat, or do you have kids...or a husband?"

I tense, looking away. Somehow, it always comes back to that, doesn't it? Every conversation, every introduction. *What do you do for a living and do you have a family?*

"No. It's just me." I bite down on the inside of my cheek, the pain keeping me focused.

"Me too."

I flick my eyes up to meet his, and he steps forward. I step back instantly, as if pushed away by some invisible force. The scent of the soup, the thoughts of my family... It's all too much.

This was a mistake.

"I'm actually going to go to bed."

"What?" He shoots a look between me and the stove. "You just started dinner."

"It just needs to simmer for about forty-five minutes.

When the carrots are soft, it's done. Can you keep an eye on it for me? I'm not... I'm not feeling too well."

I'm not lying about that, at least. My temples throb, a dull ache forming at the base of my skull. I put my hand on the back of my neck, kneading my sore muscles as I count the steps it'll take me to make it to my room. Before I take the first step, though, I know it's too late. I suck in a sharp breath seconds before everything goes black.

CHAPTER SEVENTEEN

LESSA

BEFORE

"He's so little."

Paul's warm breath is on my ear from just behind me, both hands resting on my shoulders. I nod, my eyes full of tears I don't quite understand, and I lift my hand to rest over my husband's. He presses his body into mine, saying all the things we haven't been able to say.

Our son has saved us. Maybe that's a terribly selfish thing to believe. Maybe it's not that uncommon. Either way, it's true.

He's the reason we're married. The reason we've stayed married. The reason we fought to find work and keep our apartment.

New tears prick my eyes, rolling down my cheeks with each blink.

Paul doesn't ask what's wrong—hasn't asked what's wrong in the last few hours, despite the fact that I can't bring myself to stop crying. The doctor said it's normal. That it will fade when my hormones are back under control. I'm sure he's right, but I also know it's more than that.

From the moment I turned down my parents' offer for help, from the moment I refused to leave Paul and return home, I've known my future is sealed. I've known this would be what my life looks like, even when I had no idea what it would literally look like.

Everything feels uncertain.

Confusing.

We have no real money.

Thank God I've been able to nurse the baby, because formula is outrageously expensive. In just a few short weeks, I'll be forced to return to my job at the local mall, where I'll work long hours on my feet for very little money, while my son spends his time in a day care center filled with women who smell of cigarettes and baby vomit.

This is my life, and for that little baby, I'd do anything and everything. But it still sucks.

"We should let him sleep," Paul whispers, interrupting my thoughts. He's right, I know, but I don't want to go. I don't want to leave him. Don't want to stop watching his chest rise and fall—the only assurance I have that he's still alive.

Regardless, when Paul pulls my hand, I let him lead me out into the hallway and then into the living room. I ignore my appearance in the mirror—the messy hair and pale skin, the stained clothing and unrecognizable body. It's like everything in my life has changed, including me.

In the kitchen, he pulls two frozen dinners from the

fridge and pops one into the microwave while I sift through the unopened mail on the counter.

Mostly bills, but there are cards too—from his parents who live in California, his sister, his coworkers from the new job, my coworkers, even our landlord. I recognize the hand-writing on a card near the bottom of the stack. It's addressed only to me.

I tear it open quickly, refusing to say anything for fear I'm wrong, but as I start reading, I know I'm not.

It's a simple card with a teddy bear on the front.

Inside, he's written,

We love you. We miss you. The invitation is always open.

I run a finger across the check that falls out and stare at the amount. **Ten thousand dollars.**

"What's that?" Paul raps a fork against the countertop rhythmically as he waits for our food to cook.

"It's... It's a..." I hold out the check, still speechless. The money will mean we can pay up the rent for a while, plus buy all the clothes and diapers we could need for the baby. I can even buy a breast pump, for when I return to work.

Paul moves around the counter, looking at it closer. At first, his eyes light up. "Holy shit..." Then, his expression turns cold. "No. Tear it up. We aren't accepting that."

"What? *Why?*" He can't be serious.

He flicks the paper with his fingers. "Because it's got a million strings attached, that's why."

"It does not. It's a gift. They've obviously heard we had the baby. They're trying to help."

"No, *they aren't*. They aren't helping. This is a bribe, Lessa. Tell me you see that."

"No, I don't see that." I hold out the letter. "Look. It says they love and miss me and the invitation to come home is always open. But I've already told them I'm not coming home. This is a gift and we need it. I'm not tearing it up. Forget it."

"We don't need it."

"We do. We could buy a washing machine, maybe, or fix the heat in the car. We need this money—"

He rips the check from my grasp, cutting me off. In a split second, he tears it in two. I choke back a sob of disbelief.

"*How could you—*"

He's in my face in an instant. "I'll be damned if I'm going to owe your parents a thing. They won't own me, they won't own you, and they sure as hell won't own him." He jabs a finger toward the baby's room. "End of discussion."

To further prove his point, he wads up the shredded check and shoves it into the trash, storming out of the room. I should argue, or at the very least say *something*, but there's nothing to say... Instead, I place my face in my hands and begin to sob.

CHAPTER EIGHTEEN

BLAKELY

PRESENT DAY

When I open my eyes, I'm back in my bed. The room is darker than before, illuminated only by the lamp in the corner of the room. I shoot up, grabbing for the covers.

What happened?

How did I get down here?

I stare around the room until my eyes land on what must be the answer to my questions. Tennessee is kicked back in the armchair near the fireplace across from my bed, his head drooping to the side, mouth open.

I stand up, cross the room, and nudge him.

When his eyes open, he looks as confused as I feel for half a second, and then his eyes go wide. "Oh, thank God! You're okay? How are you feeling?"

"How am I *feeling?* What do you mean?"

"I mean...you, um, you passed out. One minute you were

standing there talking to me and the next..." He feigns drop-ping to the floor dramatically. "You were out cold."

Something deep in my stomach sinks. "Oh, yeah, I...I do that."

"You *do* that? What the hell does that even mean?"

"I have a sleep condition. I pass out sometimes. It's fine." I wave my hands over my body. "I'm fine." I glance around the room. "Did you...carry me down here or something?"

"What? No. I... You don't remember?"

I shake my head, chewing my bottom lip. "Should I?"

"You walked down here yourself. I woke you up on the floor and tried to convince you to call for an ambulance, but you swore you were fine. You came down here, but you seemed out of it, so I stayed to be sure you were okay. I..." His face falls. "I didn't mean to fall asleep."

"I'm okay," I assure him, running my hands over my body as if to be sure. "Thank you for staying with me, but it's not necessary. Honestly, I'm fine." I pause. "Holy crap...what happened with dinner?"

"I turned it off when we came downstairs. I never heard from anyone, so I guess they all figured something out. I heard Lyra and Aidy get home at some point."

"What time is it?" The early morning light peeks in from under the curtain over the patio door, telling me I've been asleep for several hours with a stranger in my room.

"I..." He pats his pockets. "I have no idea, actually. My phone's still upstairs. Yours too. I think they were both lying on the counter. Let me go check."

"I'll come with you."

He pauses at the door. "Are you sure you're okay to walk up the stairs?"

"I'm fine."

Stepping back, he allows me to lead the way—I think more out of concern than chivalry, but I don't say anything. Sunlight shines in around the curtains in the small den, and when I near the stairs, I can see light up there too. I listen carefully for noise—it could be five a.m. or eleven a.m., and I wouldn't be able to tell the difference at this moment.

My head pounds as I near the top of the stairs and round the corner, staring at the pot of soup still on the stovetop. My eyes flick to the island, where I thought we left our phones, but they aren't there.

"Where did you say they were?"

Tennessee's gaze traces the countertop, his mouth dropping open. "I, um, well, I thought they were right here." He moves into the living room as I dart around the island. Could they have fallen when I passed out? Could I have grabbed them somehow without realizing it? Mine, at least? I don't remember anything else from that time, so it's certainly a possibility.

"I don't see them." He freezes in place, worry etched across his face.

"Are you positive we didn't take them downstairs?"

"Yes, I'm positive. They were right here." He's back at the island, jabbing his finger onto the granite. "I laid mine next to yours while we were cooking, and when you... er...*passed out,* I didn't grab them. I was in such a hurry to make sure you were okay and then to make sure you didn't fall down the stairs once you were awake, it was the last thing on my mind."

"You said you wanted to call for an ambulance. Did you

pick one of our phones up then, maybe?" I'm trying to jog one of our memories.

"No, there wasn't time. You were out for, like, forty-five seconds, maybe. As soon as I got around the island, you were awake and standing up. If I hadn't seen your eyes close before you fell, I would've thought you slipped."

Dammit. That would've been a good excuse too.

I force the thought away. "I'm going to check my bedroom. Maybe I put it in my pocket before I headed downstairs."

He looks apprehensive, but he doesn't argue as I dart down the stairs. "Okay, sure. I'll go with you."

"Tennessee, I'm not going to pass out again—"

"I know, but I need to find my phone too."

Before we reach my bedroom, Lyra's door swings open and she's standing in front of us, pinning me with a hard stare.

"Alright, which one of you is doing this?"

"Doing what?"

"Like you don't know."

"I *don't*."

"What's going on?" Tennessee moves to stand next to me.

Her gaze flicks to him. "What's *going on* is that while you two were in there getting cozy all night, I went and replaced the phone that went missing with a brand-new one. And what do y'know, I woke up this morning and it's missing too."

My stomach flips. "What?"

"If this is some stupid prank or—"

"Your phone is missing?" Tennessee's tone is firm. He's worried now. I think we all are.

"Yeah..." Her voice falters.

I hurry past her, into my bedroom to check the nightstand, the charger, the covers, and under the bed. When I turn around, I don't need to say anything to confirm what we all suspect. I swallow, my eyes darting between theirs.

"Someone's taken all our phones."

CHAPTER NINETEEN

LESSA

BEFORE

As I walk through the familiar front door, a wave of sadness passes through me. Sadness for all that was and all that will never be again. I'm not sure why I'm here, honestly. Not sure what I hope to gain from all of this.

What I know is that I miss my family. My parents. My home.

I want them to be part of my life again. I want to mend the bridges I once burned without looking back.

I don't know, maybe being a mother has made me sentimental, but lately, it's all I can think about.

I can't talk to Paul about it—it would turn into an all-out war. Since starting his new job, but especially since the baby was born, everything seems to set him off. The slightest question or an innocent conversation, and suddenly, he's blown a fuse. If the baby wakes him up. If the baby needs something new. If I ask him to change a diaper or help me get him to sleep. If I ask him how his day was. If I ask about our bills.

He hasn't said it yet, but I know he feels like we weren't ready for this.

And we weren't, I'll be the first to admit it. But I want to make this work. Paul's family lives far away. I've only met them a handful of times and they don't seem very close. Sometimes I feel like Paul wants to cut us off from everyone, like we're on an island alone and he's all I have.

I think it's the hormones...

I never felt this way before I was pregnant.

Mom is in the sitting room, looking over a stack of folders when I walk into the room. She glances up, obviously expecting me to be one of the staff, and her gaze falls to the baby in my arms.

She stands, her complexion blanching. "Wilson!"

"Mom..." I step forward cautiously as I hear my father's footsteps coming down the hall.

Her expression is unchanged, her eyes filled with an odd mix of disbelief and worry. "Is everything okay?"

"I'm fine. *We're* fine. I just... I wanted you to meet your grandson." I lower my arms so she can get a better look at him. He's asleep still, after crying for most of the ride over. She takes another step forward, peering at him as my father steps into the room.

"What is it, Mary Ellis? I was in the middle of—" He stops in his tracks, his face filled with an emotion I can't quite read, though he quickly composes himself. "Oh. I, um, I didn't realize you were here. Is something wrong?" He adjusts the red tie he's wearing. He's been in a meeting, I realize. Red is his power color. He only wears it when he's working on something important. Most likely, he's just walked out of his home office, leaving a few of his colleagues in there waiting for him.

"No, Dad, everything's fine. I'm here to visit. I wanted you to meet your grandson."

"We saw the announcement in the newspaper," Mom says stiffly. I can practically see her hands itching to touch him. I hold him out.

"Oh, yes, the town's been abuzz about that." Dad's tone is gruff as he unbuttons his suit jacket. "Damon!" he shouts, his voice so loud it causes Isaac to stir in my arms before I pass him to my mother.

Damon appears in the doorway in moments. "Yes, sir?"

"Can you let the men know I'll be back with them in a minute?" So, I was right. "Oh,"—he holds up a hand to stop Damon from leaving—"and could you bring us something to drink? Lemonade for the ladies, perhaps? I'll take a bourbon."

"Right away, sir."

The baby begins to fuss the second my mother takes him, and she stares at me as if it's my fault. "What's wrong with him?"

"Just bounce him." I try to show her how it's done. Truth be told, I've always suspected my mother had very little to do with me as an infant—there aren't many pictures of either of my parents holding me at that point—and the awkward way she tries to bounce him further proves my theory. "Here, he likes to be patted. Try putting him against your chest and—"

"*Against my chest?*" She looks horrified, glancing down at her patterned shirt. "My dear, this blouse is genuine silk." She holds him out for me with disgust.

I reach to take him back, her words cutting through me, when my father extends his arms, hands outstretched.

"May I?" he asks.

I lean back, allowing him to take Isaac. He stares down at him for a moment, his Adam's apple bobbing with a hard swallow before he places him against his shoulder and begins to rock. His grip on my son doesn't look comfortable for either of them, his body rigid and awkward, but he's trying. That's all I can ask for.

I smile at him, his gesture bringing tears to my eyes just as Damon reappears with a tray of our drinks. Mom hands me one, then takes one for herself. She's watching me with a suspicious gaze. Waiting for me to admit the real reason I'm here, perhaps.

She sits back in the chair, lifting one leg to cross over the other, and smoothing her hand over her tweed pant leg. "So, are you going to tell us how you've been?"

"Oh, you know, it's an adjustment, of course. But I'm fine. Isaac's growing like a weed. His doctor says he's healthy and right on track. And he should be. He eats constantly." I laugh, but when they don't join in, I clear my throat and change the subject. "How are you guys?"

"Oh, well, the Templetons are having their annual garden party this weekend, and Tish is just a mess with trying to plan it all while Brian's out of town, so I've been helping with that." Mom sips her lemonade, looking positively joyous. "And...did you hear the Johnsons are getting a divorce? Rumor has it he slept with his tennis instructor." She shrugs. "So, same old same old, I guess. Oh,"—she purses her lips, looking at my dad—"and...did you tell her?"

Dad shakes his head, still *shh*-ing in the baby's ear.

"Your father traded in the yacht for one double the size. We're thinking of sailing around the coast next summer." She glances between me and the baby. "He'll be old enough to join us by then, won't he?"

It's the first sign of the wall coming down. The first invitation to be part of their lives again.

"Um, yeah, maybe. He should be."

"If not, we could always hire a nanny to stay here with him. The Gormans' daughter has nearly outgrown hers, so maybe we could snatch her up before she finds employment elsewhere."

The very thought is terrifying. I'm already dreading leaving him for the few hours a day I'll have to be at work. I can't imagine leaving him for an entire year. "No, that won't be necessary. He'll be old enough."

"Marvelous." She leans forward to set her drink down on a marble coaster. "Sweetheart, we really have missed you."

"I've missed you guys, too." The statement comes out as a breath of relief.

"So," my father says in a low whisper, trying not to disturb the baby as he finally calms down, "do you have your things in the car, or should we send someone to get them?"

"What?" Cold washes over me.

"Your things, darling." Mom waves her hand in the air like a pageant queen. "I know you didn't take much with you, but surely you have a few things you'll want to bring home. Of course, we could just replace them if you'd rather do that."

"Wait, no. I'm not... Mom, I told you I was just here to visit. I'm not moving back home."

The air is sucked from the room. As if he senses it, Isaac's cry tears through the house again. My father tenses, and he stops rocking at once. "You're not?"

"I just wanted you to meet your grandson..." I recognize my mistake in seconds. Something shifts in both of their expressions. There were no walls coming down, no invitations being extended. Nothing will change unless I give them exactly what they want. There are no compromises with my parents. Never have been.

"I thought I was clear about this." My father stands, and my mother moves to join him. As always, they're a united front. He hands Isaac back to me.

"Dad, please! Don't do this. I just... I don't want to lose you. I still want to see you, for you to see him."

"You made your choice, Lessa Elizabeth." His voice is calm but firm. There will be no changing his mind. It's one I've heard him use in business negotiations more times than I can count. "Now, you must live with the consequences."

"Just like that?" I shake my head. "You'd really just abandon your own daughter? Your own blood?" Tears stream down my cheeks, but I don't bother to dry them. Let them see what they've done to me. It's the only power I have left.

"It's the other way around. *You* abandoned *us*." The words are sharp on his tongue. "You will always have a place here, should you choose to accept it, but as long as you're with...*him*..." He casts a disgusted look at the doorway. "You're not welcome in our lives. The choice will always remain with you. But do not test my patience." He grips Mom's hand. "*Damon!*"

Without another glance my way, they turn and strut from the room.

Damon appears in the doorway with an apologetic frown. "I'm sorry, Miss Astor. I have to see you out now."

"Don't bother, Damon. Thank you, but I can find the door myself." I swipe a finger under my eyes, drying my tears as I move past him. Trying to quiet my son as I make my way down the hall and out the door, my body trembles with anger.

I don't cry the rest of the way home, my sadness replaced with outright rage.

How dare they do this to me?

How dare they act like I'm so dispensable?

ONCE BACK HOME, I'm shocked to see Paul's tool bag on the floor of our apartment. He's not meant to be home for a few hours.

"Paul?"

"Where were you?"

I jolt at the sound of his voice behind me.

I whip around, a hand to my chest. "Oh, God, you scared me. I took Isaac for a drive. What are you already doing home?"

"Did you go see them?" His jaw is tight.

"I..."

"Answer me!" he screams. "You did, didn't you?"

"Let me go put him down, okay?" He's too close to me. I can hardly breathe in the tiny hallway, and my body's drenched in sweat.

"You thought you wouldn't get caught. You thought you were so slick." He follows me down the hall, taunting me like a schoolyard bully. "But I called to check on you during my lunch and you didn't answer. Called a few more times, then decided to come home and make sure everything was okay."

I push open the nursery door and place Isaac into his crib, careful not to wake him.

"Imagine my surprise when you weren't even here."

I walk past him, but he grabs my arm, his grip tight enough to make me scream. "Stop it!" I pull away. "Please. I'll explain, just not in here. Let him sleep."

He follows me out into the hall, and the second the door is closed, he shoves me into the wall and presses his forehead into mine with so much force, I cry out. "Did you go to see them?"

"Paul, please..."

"*Fucking answer me!*" He pounds his fists into the wall on either side of me, and I yelp.

The noise wakes Isaac, and he begins to cry. "Please. I need to check on him."

Paul grabs my arms, jerking me forward. I bend backward under the weight of him. "You know how I feel about your parents. You know what they've done. They cost me a job. They tried to take you away from me."

"I would never leave you, Paul. They know that. *You* know that. Haven't I proven it by now?"

He shakes his head, clicking his tongue. "Yeah, maybe yesterday I would've said you had, but right now, I don't feel like I know you at all."

"It was just a visit. I just wanted them to meet their grandson—"

He cuts off my words with a slap to the cheek. It's the first time he's ever slapped me. There've been close calls, but this time, there's a line drawn in the sand. He lowers his face to mine. *"You* chose *me.* I never made you. I told you this wasn't the life you should've lived, but you chose me. And now, you're stuck with me. Do you understand? It's you, me, and him, forever." He backs up half a step. "Don't let me catch you forgetting that again."

As he walks away, I suck in a sharp breath and lift a hand to my cheek. The heat under my palm is proof of what happened—proof that he hit me—and yet, I still feel like I must've imagined it. How could he want to hurt me? How can any of this be real? My vision blurs with tears just before Isaac's cries bring me back to reality. I rush into his room, hoping the sounds of his sobs will drown out my own.

CHAPTER TWENTY

BLAKELY

PRESENT DAY

"How could someone have taken all our phones? It's not possible." Tennessee follows closely behind me as I jog up the stairs.

I turn back to look at him. "I have no idea, but why else aren't they here? We didn't all somehow just simultaneously misplace them."

"No, someone took them," Lyra says from the front of the line. "Just like someone's been taking my stuff all week."

"But who?" I ask as we near the main floor.

"What's going on?" Daniel pauses from pouring a cup of orange juice to stare at us.

"Do you have your phone?" Lyra asks.

Aidy stirs a bowl of oatmeal from her seat at the kitchen island. "Why? Where's yours?"

"Missing. *Again.*" Lyra walks across the room, resting a hand on the counter. "Do either of you have yours?"

"Sure." Aidy hops down from the barstool. "Do you want me to call it?"

"None of us can find ours," I cut in. "They're all missing."

"What?" Daniel sets the bottle of orange juice down, glancing toward the stairs that lead to his bedroom.

"Do you have yours?" Tennessee asks.

"Uh, yeah. At least, I think so. It's in my room." He moves past us, making his way up the stairs as Aidy walks down the hall into her bedroom.

From where I stand, I watch as she stops to glance down at the end table. She picks up the novel lying there, then checks the floor before looking back at us. "It was right here. I left it on the charger."

She spins around, lifts her pillows and sheets, and drops them back down. Then, a sly smile crosses her face. "Wait a second. Ha ha. This is some kind of a joke, right? Where did you guys put it?"

"It's not a joke." I shake my head. "Someone has taken all of our phones."

"But it's impossible. Who would do that? It has to be one of us. A prank, like Aidy said." Tennessee paces the floor, chewing on his thumbnail as he thinks aloud. "Someone here is doing this."

"My money's on you, trying to make us think it's this damn ghost." Lyra casts an accusing look at Tennessee.

"What? No. I'm not doing this, I swear!"

"Seems awful convenient you'd bring up this *supposed* murder and then, suddenly, things start to go missing."

"Your notes were missing before he brought up the murder. And everything he told us about the place is true."

Every eye in the room falls to me. "I looked it up. He wasn't lying."

"I never said he was lying and, anyway, it seems fitting you'd remember when the notes went missing, since you're the one who conveniently found them. For all I know, the two of you are working together to freak the rest of us out."

"Our phones are missing, too." Tennessee stops in his tracks, shaking his head. "We have nothing to do with this."

"They're all missing." The voice comes from behind us, and we turn to find Daniel standing there, hands dropped to his sides, chest rising and falling with heavy breaths. "I can't find mine either."

I shake my head. "We need to go to the police."

"What are you talking about?" Daniel frowns. "Why? This is obviously some stupid prank. Someone just needs to tell us where they are. This isn't funny."

"What if it's not a prank? No one's coming clean. If none of us stole the phones, someone else must've come in here and taken them. We need to report it," I say.

"She's right." Tennessee steps toward me. "If someone is doing this, it's time for the joke to be over. Tell us the truth now, or we'll have no choice but to go to the police."

Everyone exchanges glances, but no one says a word.

Finally, Tennessee goes on, "Then, I agree with Blakely. What choice do we have but to go to the police? Although, maybe we should contact the property manager first."

"Why?" Daniel asks.

"I was just thinking that maybe someone still has the code to this place. Like an old tenant. If that's the case, maybe they will want to give that information to the police."

"Doubtful," Lyra says, "since that would just get them in

trouble for putting us in danger. I'm *so* not leaving this place a good review."

I nod. "It's not a bad idea to contact the property manager. Lucy's her name. She gave me her number when she came over to look at the hot tub. It's hanging on the fridge upstairs. Which, actually now that I think about it, someone was supposed to show up to fix the hot tub on Tuesday or Wednesday, but we never heard from anyone. We should touch base with Lucy and let her know that, anyway. And then we can tell her what's going on with our phones and see what she thinks."

"Okay, but how are we going to call her?" Lyra asks, a hand on her hip. I'm not entirely sure she's against the idea, but we haven't convinced her just yet, either. "We have no phones, remember?"

"Oh. Right."

"We could walk." Tennessee points to the door. "The office is just supposed to be, like, a block away, right?"

"You and Aidy never went to find it?" I ask, recalling their earlier conversation.

"No. We never got around to it." He runs a finger over his bottom lip, pinching it thoughtfully. "But we can now. We could just walk down there and talk to whoever's working."

"Or drive," Lyra says. "Aidy can drive us all. Then we can go to the police with whatever information they give us. If someone has the code, I'm contacting my attorney. Talk about an invasion of privacy."

"Agreed," Daniel says, running a hand through his hair. "Let's get going, though. I want this sorted sooner rather than later."

We break apart, moving to our rooms to get ready, and then meet by the front door. Aidy swings her keys around her finger as she waits for us. As a stark juxtaposition to the loudly patterned jumpsuit she's wearing, she's being extra quiet. For the first time since we met, her face seems lifeless and pale, her head hanging down. This place is really starting to get to us all.

When she looks up and catches me staring, she asks, "Do you really think someone could've broken in without anyone noticing?"

It's a question that lingers with me. In truth, *no*. I don't believe that. I don't understand how anyone could've come into the house and made it to all of the various rooms quickly enough to take our phones without someone seeing them. But where does it leave us, if that's not the case? It means it was an inside job. The monster's inside the house.

So who can we trust?

I look around. These people are practically strangers. Just days ago, I barely knew them. In a lot of ways, that's still the case. I don't trust easily, not after what I've been through, so I'm at a loss now. Who can I trust, if anyone? And if no one, what should I do? What if they're all against me?

As we make our way outside, down the stairs, and to the driveway, Aidy and Daniel stop so quickly I nearly slam into them.

"No, no, no, no, no..." Aidy rushes toward the Toyota, but we can all see from here what she's looking at. The car in the driveway sits on its rims. All four tires have been slashed.

"It's okay," I try to assure her. She looks ready to burst into tears. "We just need to contact the rental company. They should be able to send someone out to replace them."

"We have no way to call anyone," she whimpers. "How much is this going to cost? I spent almost everything I had saved getting here. The flight, the car..."

"I don't know," I say. "It shouldn't be too much, hopefully. The insurance may cover it. Here, let's just take my car, okay? We'll get to the office and see what's going on—"

"That's not going to be possible." I look up to see Daniel standing on the other side of Aidy's car, staring down at mine with a grimace. "Actually, it looks like none of us will be driving anywhere for a while. As it stands, all three cars are out of commission."

I leave Aidy to check it out, just to discover he's right. All three cars—Aidy's, Tennessee's, and mine—have had their tires slashed.

"Someone did this on purpose," I say, my throat growing dry. "They took our phones and they slashed our tires. Guys, what the hell is going on?"

"I don't know, but I think at this point we're all in agreement. We need to get to the police." Daniel starts to move back to the house.

"But how?" I call after him. "We have no phones. No way to leave."

"Oh. But we still have our laptops." Lyra rushes past me. "We can send a message to a towing company, or a cab company, something."

Following her inside, Tennessee hurries toward his room. "I'll do it. I can send my mom a message. She'll have a phone." He grabs his laptop and returns as we all gather around him. "Okay, here we go." He pulls up his social media and types out a quick message, then looks up at us, drumming his fingers on the countertop as we wait.

Within a few minutes, a chime notifies us she's responded. "Okay, she's called the nonemergency number and a tow company to come out and check on us." Leaning down, he squints at the screen. "She says they told her it could be a few hours before they get here."

Lyra groans. "Perfect."

"Could she just come get us?" Aidy asks. "Would that be faster?"

"She's in her seventies and not in the best health," Tennessee says hesitantly. "She can't really drive anymore."

"It'll be fine. In the meantime, some of us should try to walk down to the office," I point out. "It was the original plan, and I still think it's a good one. If they have information that could help the police find out who did this, I want to know." I don't say it aloud, but I also know I'll feel better if we can make contact with other people. Safety in numbers and all that.

"Yeah, but if we leave, we won't have a way to know if the police get here," Aidy says. "Maybe we should just stay here instead and let the police handle it. We could tell them our theory and let them follow up if they think it's worth it."

"No, Blakely's right," Tennessee says. "We don't have time to waste. We should split up. Half of us can go to the office, half of us should wait here for the police."

"Well, if y'all are so ready to volunteer, by all means..." Lyra says, gesturing toward the door. "As for me, I'm sitting my butt right here and waiting until the police get here. No need to play armchair detective."

I look at Tennessee, who nods softly. "I'll go if you will."

It's not what I want to do. Walking through the woods after what we've been through today—especially with no phones—sounds terrifying, but I'm not sure staying here sounds any better.

"Fine. Daniel, Aidy, what about you? Are you going or staying?"

"I'll stay with Lyra." Aidy takes a small step toward her.

"Yeah, me too," Daniel says. "I have a bad knee, and I've already promised my orthopedist I wouldn't come home with any new injuries from this trip. Walking through the woods right now seems like a bad idea."

I nod, looking at Tennessee. "Fine. Just us then."

He grabs two bottles of water from the fridge while I change into more comfortable shoes and, together, we head for the door. The air is cooler than I expected and I immediately shiver as it meets my skin. There's a fog rolling in over the hills around us, which only makes us feel more cut off from the rest of the world.

He passes me my water as we make our way up the hill, trying to get a clear view of the woods around us. The wind howls through the trees, whipping my hair in every direction.

"Okay, so if I'm remembering right, the letter said to cut through the woods behind the house." He checks the house, then points toward the woods. "So, I'd say this is behind, which means I'm guessing the office is up this way?" He points straight ahead. "Or maybe back this way? What do you think?"

"This is the direction we saw that light from the first night." I point toward the wooded path, despite everything in my gut telling me this is a bad decision. "So, let's try this way first."

He nods, jogging to catch up with me as I move forward, my legs already burning from the steep climb. The tree branches are barer today than they were when we first arrived, the evidence of their loss scattered across the ground.

"Well, this isn't exactly how we expected to spend our peaceful, quiet retreat, is it?"

I laugh at the absurdity of his statement. "No, I guess not."

"I mean, if they're going for the whole real-life action hero thing, they've got it in the bag. They could be catering toward an entirely different kind of escape."

I smile and shake my head. "You're not wrong." When we aren't talking, the forest is almost painfully quiet. Except for the sound of the crunching leaves under our feet, there's virtually no other noise out here. "I think I'm going to leave after we get the cars fixed."

"What?"

I think I've shocked us both by saying it aloud. "Yeah, I... I should've gotten a lot more work in than I have. Being here has been more of a distraction than anything. And, whatever's going on with our phones and cars... I just don't think it's good for me to be here anymore."

"But it'll be taken care of now that we're getting the police involved, right? Come on, you can't let whoever's behind this ruin your trip. You're the one who said you needed this at the beginning of the week, didn't you?"

"I thought I did, yeah, but I'm here for the wrong reasons."

"And what reasons would that be?"

I press my lips together, shoving my hands into the pockets of my hoodie. "It doesn't matter."

"Blakely..." He stops in his tracks, forcing me to stop too.

His eyes find mine from a few feet away. "You can talk to me. You know that, right? I don't know what's going on with you, but...I'm here, okay?"

I break our eye contact and continue walking. "Don't be so dramatic. There's nothing to talk about. I just don't feel like staying here and getting murdered."

He groans, jogging to keep up with me. "Well, how about I promise to keep you safe?"

I grimace. "If you'd have read my books, you'd know I prefer for women to save themselves."

Without missing a beat, he retorts, "Well, fine, then *you* can keep *me* safe. How about that?"

Releasing a loud groan, I drop my head forward. "Has anyone ever told you you're impossible?"

"It's what I hear." He catches my eye. "And anyway, this is just a one-off. I'm sure it's either someone in the house or maybe, worst case, an old tenant. All our phones are protected with passcodes, surely. And now that the police are involved, no one should bother us. This is a really safe area, despite the history of this particular house. Like, it's the kind of place where people leave their doors unlocked and kids run and play in the neighborhood, and no one bats an eye."

"That sounds...a little too good to be true." We move through a clearing, then through a narrow path of trees, careful not to trip on the overgrown vines catching on the fabric of our pants.

Once the path has become less treacherous, Tennessee clears his throat. "I used to think that's what I wanted, you know?"

"What's that?"

"Kids. Safety. A family. The whole nine yards."

I swallow, my throat suddenly tight, but luckily, he doesn't seem to notice my discomfort.

"But it wasn't in the cards."

There's a ringing in my ears suddenly, and I stop midstep, grabbing onto a tree to steady myself.

"Whoa, hey, hey..." Tennessee is at my side in an instant, arms outstretched to keep me from falling. "Are you okay? What happened? What's wrong?"

"I'm fine. I tripped over a tree root, I think." I release the tree to prove my point, trying desperately not to sway as I blink the dark specks from my vision. "I'm good, I swear." I take a half step and stumble, reaching for the tree again. Tears blur my vision.

"Whoa, hang on." He stops me before I can try to walk off again. "You're obviously *not* good. What's going on with you? You look like you've seen a ghost."

I fight down bile as it rises in my chest. I can't tell him. I can't tell anyone. And yet, I find myself clawing at the words as they move toward my throat.

"Blakely, come on. You're scaring me."

A stray tear trickles down my cheek, and I brush it away as soon as I feel it.

"Did I say something? Did something happen?"

"I'm fine, Tennessee. Can we please just drop it?"

He steps back, both hands up in surrender. "Yeah, okay. We can. But you have to sit down for a second."

"What? No. We have to keep walking. We have to find the office. We don't have time for this."

"We aren't going to find anything right now, okay? You can hardly walk. You look like you're about to pass out at any second, and I'm not sure I'm going to be able to carry you all the way back down the hill. So, I need you alive and well and capable of getting yourself places. Which means right now, you need to sit down and breathe."

"I don't like people who tell me what to do." Despite what I'm saying, I find myself easing down against the tree trunk.

"Yeah, well, I like people who stay conscious."

I slide my feet out from under me, my breathing slowing as I hit the ground. To my surprise, Tennessee sits down across from me. He picks up a leaf and twirls it between his fingers aimlessly, his gaze flicking up to check on me every once in a while.

I appreciate the fact that he's not pushing me, though I know he wants to. I'm not trying to be difficult, despite how I know it seems, but I can't talk to him about this.

About them.

I just can't.

"You don't have to tell me what's going on. I get it—we're not friends. We hardly know each other. But can you at least tell me... Should I be worried? Like, are you going to pass out again or..."

"I told you I'm fine."

His head falls, his gaze returning to the leaf in his hands, as guilt eats away at me. He's only trying to help. I see and appreciate that.

"It's just stress."

His eyes find mine again, new hope in them.

"Stress causes me to...to black out, I guess. It's not a big deal. I promise, I'm fine. And I'm calm."

"You don't look calm."

"*I am,*" I say forcefully, then lower my voice. "I swear I am."

He nods. "Okay, fine. Whatever you say." After a moment, he adds, "I used to chew my nails when I was stressed."

I snort, the words surprising me so much my head falls back against the tree with laughter. I needed this. Needed to laugh. Needed to forget the stress of this week. The mission. The pressure to get it right.

I adjust on the ground, meeting his eyes finally. "I used to want a family, too."

"Yeah?" His brows lift with interest.

"Yeah." I squeeze my eyes shut. This is probably a mistake. "Actually, I had a son. And a husband, too."

When my eyes pop open, he's staring at me expectantly. "*Had?*"

"I lost them both."

He cocks his head to the side, tossing the leaf down. "I'm really sorry, Blakely. I had no idea."

"I don't talk about it—*them*—much. It's still too hard, y'know?"

"Yeah, I get that for sure."

I clear my throat. "The blackouts started after I lost them. Whenever I get too upset or stressed... It's usually just a few seconds. My doctors can't quite figure it out."

"That sounds really scary."

"Not really. There's nothing scarier than what I've already been through."

He draws his lips in on one side. "Can I ask what...what happened?"

"Car accident," I say simply. It's easier than the truth.

He shakes his head, avoiding my eyes. "That's... God, I can't... I'm sorry. That's awful."

"He was four years old." Now that I've started talking about it, I can't bring myself to stop. "I didn't even get to know him yet." I dry my cheek on my shoulder. "Anyway, this week is the anniversary of... Well, it was yesterday, actually. I just couldn't be at home this week. I needed to be somewhere else. Anywhere else."

"I get that." His voice is soft.

"Please don't mention it to the others. I don't want to talk about them with strangers."

"Of course." A sly smile spreads on his lips. "Does that mean we're friends now?"

I toss a twig at him. "Don't press your luc—" Something catches my eye just beyond where we're sitting and I cock my head to the side. "Hey, what's that?"

He spins around quickly, as if ready to attack, then his shoulders fall. "What's what? I don't see anything."

I push up from the tree, steadying myself before I walk toward what I'm staring at. Tennessee's right beside me, an arm out in case I need it as we make our way several feet to our left.

"There." I bend over, running my hands over the large, circular piece of rusty metal.

"What is that?" Tennessee bends down next to me, using both hands to clear the pine needles and dry leaves away from it. "It looks like...a hatch of some sort. Like a bunker."

"A storm shelter, maybe?" I ask. There's no writing on the door—just a simple handle that sticks up an inch or two. It was what had originally caught my eye, leading me to notice the perfect circle in the dead grass. The metal has corroded with age. "Should we try to open it?"

"Yeah, maybe." Tennessee grips the handle and gives it a firm tug.

Nothing.

He pulls again, this time hard enough to release a groan, but the door doesn't budge. "It's either locked or so rusted it won't open."

I look around. "Maybe it doesn't even belong to the owner of the property. Maybe it's been forgotten about. This could hold, like...some old secrets or buried treasure or something."

"Old secrets and buried treasure, hmm?" He laughs. "More like old cans of corn and evaporated milk, maybe."

"Okay, so I've watched *National Treasure* one too many times. Sue me." I grip the handle with him. "One more time." Together, we summon all our strength, tugging on the metal until my hands burn for relief, but to no avail.

The door doesn't budge an inch.

"Oh, well. Worth a try." Tennessee dusts off his hands, breathing heavily. "We should probably get back to our search for the office, if you're okay? Only one treasure hunt at a time."

We turn away from the bunker and retreat back up over the hill, but this time, Tennessee keeps in step with me, making sure I don't fall.

The bunker was a nice distraction, but I'm glad to be back focused on what really matters. Finding the office, finding answers, and finding my way back home before anyone discovers my secret.

CHAPTER TWENTY-ONE

LESSA

BEFORE

I'm going to leave him.

It's a promise I make to myself and to Isaac every night before bed. Paul is no longer the man I married. Or maybe he was always this man and I failed to see it. Either way, this isn't the marriage I signed up for.

Once upon a time, he made me laugh. He was kind. Gentle. Caring. He saw me, loved me, and chose me, not because of who my family is or because of what I could offer him, but instead because of who I am.

I've never been able to say that about any of my past boyfriends.

Never been able to outrun my last name in this town.

But still, even with everything he had going for him, all the cards in his favor, he managed to disappoint me anyway.

"You won't do that, will you?" I ask Isaac, kissing his

fingers. "You won't disappoint me, will you? You're the only man in my life I can count on."

He stares up at me from the crib, blissfully unaware of what's going on. I smile down at him, running a finger across his cheek. "It's all going to be okay."

With that promise in mind, I turn to his closet and dig toward the back until I find the suitcase I've hidden. Inside, I have nearly a thousand dollars in cash, plus a few outfits and shoes packed for the both of us.

When the time comes, we're going to run and we're never looking back. I shove two more ten-dollar bills I was able to snag from Paul's wallet earlier into the stack of cash and close the suitcase, shoving it toward the back of the closet and covering it with his bouncy seat, a pack of diapers, and a few stacks of clothes he's outgrown.

I slide the closet door shut just as I hear the shower turn off down the hall.

Moments later, his heavy footsteps send my heart thudding. I make my way back to the crib just before the bedroom door opens and he peers in. Can he see the terror on my face? The guilt? I hope not.

Before I can turn to look at him, the phone rings in the kitchen.

"I'll get it—" I start to say, moving for the door, but he's faster. He reaches the phone quickly, turning away as he talks to the caller in a hushed tone. I stare at the droplets of water on his bare back, dripping down from his hair as he speaks.

Within seconds, the call ends and he turns back to me with a grin spread across his lips.

"What is it?" I ask. He looks genuinely happy, a look I haven't seen from him in what feels like ages.

"We got it." His hands shoot out to his sides, and he rushes toward me, gathering me in a hug. The dampness of his body seeps into my clothes, making me hot, sticky, and uncomfortable. Not to mention confused.

"Got what?"

"The house." He pulls back, adjusting the towel around his waist and running one hand over my hair. "We got it."

My heart sinks. "But...how?"

We weren't supposed to get it. Two months ago, he mentioned finding a house he thought I'd love, one he believed he could fix up for us over time. It was a shack, the way he'd described it, in desperate need of renovations. I'd said very little, from what I can recall, maybe just *okay*, because I had no real choice. He wasn't asking, he was telling. But I never actually believed it would happen.

I never actually believed we'd be approved. We are dirt poor—hardly making ends meet as it is. How could anyone ever think we deserve to be homeowners?

I mask the panic on my face, forcing a smile, and pull him into another hug solely to keep him from reading any of the apprehension I'm feeling.

"Everything's going to be okay now," he promises, kissing my cheek. His grip tightens on my sides, and I hug him tighter, praying he can't feel my racing heart. "Everything's going to be okay."

CHAPTER TWENTY-TWO

BLAKELY

PRESENT DAY

M y legs burn for relief as we reach the top of the hill. The wind has cooled the afternoon air considerably, the sky growing dark with promises of an afternoon storm.

Just as I'm preparing to suggest we turn around and try the other way, a road in the distance comes into view. We step onto it and I squint, leaning forward to try to get a better look at a large house in the distance. "Wait a second. Is that it?"

"Something, yeah." Tennessee picks up his pace, and I rush to keep up with him.

The house is two stories tall with wood siding and a balcony running the length of the top floor. It looks like the sort of cabin you'd expect to find in the woods, I guess. Nothing particularly special about it.

There are two cars in the parking lot: a red minivan and

a gray SUV. We pass by them on our way toward the entrance, guided by a sign that points up the stairs. **Office,** it reads. In the back, there's a vacant swimming pool, with a single float spinning lazy circles in the water. It's too cold for swimming now, has been for weeks, as evidenced by the lower-than-usual water level, tinged a shade of seafoam green.

Tennessee grabs the storm door and pulls it open for me.

We step inside the small space. It smells strange in here —enough to make me breathe through my mouth rather than my nose—but the place looks newly renovated with hardwood floors throughout and floor-to-ceiling windows. There's a small, executive-style desk in the center of the room, with an office chair behind it.

"Hello?" Tennessee calls softly, his voice echoing through the quiet space.

Beyond the desk, there's a door with a sign that reads, **Employees Only.**

"Is anyone here?" he adds, after a few moments with no response.

"Maybe we should check downstairs?" I suggest. It's quiet up here, too quiet, and I desperately rub away the chills that have lined my arms.

"Sure." He nods, looking as relieved as I feel to be getting out of this room. We exit the building and head back down the stairs. The bottom floor has a set of large French doors. We push them open and the lights inside flick on, obviously triggered by our motion.

Like the welcome letter promised, the downstairs is a single, open room with two pool tables, a bar, several couches and televisions, and a few high-top tables. The back doors lead to the pool area, which we can see even more clearly from here.

The room is empty, stale almost.

"How long has it been since anyone was here?" I wonder aloud.

"The letter mentioned other properties, didn't it? I mean, our property can't be the only one they manage. There's too much stuff here."

"I agree. So why isn't there anyone here *using* the stuff?"

He shakes his head, moving forward to examine the pool table as I walk the length of the room. When I reach the kitchen, a thought occurs to me. "Oh, wait. You know what? We should go back upstairs and use the office phone to try and call our phones."

"Why? You think they're here?"

"No..." The thought hadn't occurred to me. "No, but maybe someone in the house will hear them. Or maybe someone will answer. Or maybe they're turned off. I just think we should at least try."

"Okay, sure." He doesn't seem entirely convinced, but he follows my lead anyway as I exit the clubhouse space and move back toward the office upstairs.

Once inside, I knock loudly on the desk. "Hello? Anyone here?" I call.

Tennessee shrugs one shoulder. "Maybe they went out for lunch."

With that thought, I inhale deeply and make my way around the desk, lifting the phone to my ear. I press the switch hook, waiting for a dial tone.

After a few moments, I pull the receiver away and stare at it. "Nothing."

"No answer?" Tennessee's brows draw down.

"No, I mean it's not working. There's no dial tone. Nothing." I shove my finger into the button over and over before slamming the phone down. "Dammit. I don't understand what's happening."

Next to me, Tennessee is looking through the papers on the desk. He shoves the keyboard out of the way. "Hey, hey... Lookee what we have here."

I lean down, spying a username and password underneath a name: **Cindy.**

"Thank you, Cindy." Tennessee sits down in the chair, tapping buttons on the keyboard until the computer screen lights up.

"Are you sure about this?"

"Well, obviously no one's here, so the least we can do is do some investigation into what's going on." He types in the password, and I hold my breath. In a second, the screen changes. "We're in. What should I check first?"

"How should I know? Do they have, like, a company mainframe or something?"

He pokes around, opening this and that, before he lands on her inbox. "Here we go..." He scrolls through the emails, most of which are simple exchanges between coworkers about housekeeping dates and repairs. "Okay, so, yeah, they definitely have several properties." He clicks on a message, then another. "Hey, wait, look at this."

I lean down closer to the screen to try to get a good look at what he's reading.

"It was sent two days before we arrived. She says they

had an emergency come up with the property on Dayton Street. They had to cancel the reservation until it was fixed."

"So?"

"So..." He clicks out of the email and scrolls to another one, one he's already read. "That's exactly what this one said. An emergency on McHaney Street." He backs out of the email and continues to scroll, then nods. "Emergency on Jane Drive."

"What do you think happened?"

He continues to scroll through her outbox. "She sent eighteen emails that day. It looks like all of their reservations were canceled..." He glances over his shoulder to look at me. "All except ours."

"What does that mean?"

"I have no idea, but it explains why there's no one here."

A new thought occurs to me. "Hey, can you search for Lucy in her inbox?"

"Lucy?" He does as I've asked.

"Remember? She's the manager here. I told you guys earlier she came by when we were having trouble with the hot tub."

"Oh, right. Yeah."

Recalling the conversation we had, I bob my head with a sudden realization. "Actually, now that I think about it, she said they were having trouble with their phones. Maybe there's an email from her that explains what's going on... Maybe one of those cars out there is hers."

He completes the search and shakes his head. "There are no emails from anyone named Lucy. Lucille, maybe?" He types it in. "No. Nothing. Did you get her last name?"

"No." Disappointment mixes with worry in my core. "We should go back."

"Yeah, okay." When he stands, the heat kicks on, and suddenly, I'm hit with a putrid smell. It's the smell I noticed when we first entered the room, but now it's a million times more pungent. I cover my nose with the back of my hand as Tennessee gags. My vision blurs with tears, the scent stinging my eyes.

"Holy crap. What is that?" I lift my shirt to cover my nose and mouth, shooting looks this way and that.

"I have...no idea," he says through his coughing fit.

Then, all at once, it hits me. Like the scent of a mouse that climbed into the wall of my first apartment and died. Only bigger. Much, much bigger.

Tennessee is already headed for the door when I speak, stopping him in his tracks.

"Tennessee, something's dead in here."

He spins around, his shirt pinched up over his nose. "What?"

I glance toward the door marked only for employees. It's the only option. The only place we haven't checked.

"No." He pales.

"It has to be. You don't have to check with me. You can stand outside."

He shakes his head. "No way. We should get the police. If you're right, you could be messing with a crime scene."

I'm already walking toward the door, though, my hand outstretched for the handle. I need to know if I'm right. I need to know what we're dealing with.

I turn the knob, half expecting it to be locked, but to my surprise, it opens without any trouble. I push open the door slowly and the scent fills my nostrils. It burns my eyes and my lungs, making me gag, but even as my vision blurs with tears, I know I'll never be able to unsee what's in this room. Nothing could've prepared me for the sight waiting for me.

However bad I thought it might be to begin with, this is so much worse.

CHAPTER TWENTY-THREE

LESSA

BEFORE

The first few months in the house, Paul is on his best behavior. He only touches me like he used to—full of love and tenderness. He's proud of himself. Happy we're here. He thinks I've forgotten what the monster inside him looks like.

Still, we go through the motions and pretend everything's okay.

Isaac is crawling now, moving around like he's constantly on a mission. Paul loves him, I think. I truly believe he does. Maybe more than he loves me. Occasionally, he'll get down on the floor and hold his toys in front of him, or walk through the house bouncing him to calm his fussing. It's more than some of my coworkers' husbands do, and they tell me I shouldn't complain.

They're right, I guess. He's trying. I can appreciate that. None of us are perfect, and I'd never expect him to be. But, try as I might, I can't forget the months of living in fear. I can't forget the way my cheek burned when his palm connected with it. I can't forget the times he grabbed me too tightly or shoved me into walls.

I can't forget the suitcase now stored in Isaac's new room, just waiting for me to make my move.

Over dinner that evening, Paul talks about the bathroom renovations he's going to do once spring gets here. After we get our income tax check. A bathtub, for starters—since we're currently bathing Isaac in the sink—a faucet that doesn't leak when you use it, and new flooring to replace the cracked tile.

"This place could be a real beauty," he says, picking food from his teeth as he stares around.

He sees it, I guess. Sees the vision. The final product.

Maybe I do too, in a way. It has charm. With just a bit of money, it could be something special. But a house is only as good as the people inside of it. And right now, we are far from good.

Isaac begins fussing, and I offer him more of the mashed green beans.

"You're quiet tonight," Paul says, eyeing me from across the table.

"Hmm? Sorry. Just...lost in thought, I guess."

"What's there to think about?"

"Work, mostly."

"Busy today or somethin'?"

I nod, spooning more green beans into Isaac's mouth.

"Oh, by the way, I was looking for one of his baby pictures for Mom earlier while you were in the shower, and I checked in his closet."

I freeze at his words, at the tone with which they're spoken.

"W-which picture?"

"One of her and him when she came to visit." He shrugs. "I didn't find the picture, but...well, I'm sure you can guess what I did find."

My heart pounds in my ears, and I try my hardest not to react. I place the spoon down and turn my complete attention to my husband. "What's that?"

He shoves his plate away from him, a wry grin on his greasy lips. "Going to play dumb, hmm?"

"I don't know what you mean." I stand, grabbing my plate and moving to the sink.

He stands from his place. "Are you planning to leave me? Is that what this is about? After all I've done for you?"

"I'm not planning to leave you, Paul. Don't be silly." I can't bring myself to look at him; I can hardly take a breath.

"Then why do you have a suitcase full of cash in the closet?" He rushes around the table, catching my arm. "Cash that could've been used to fix up this house."

He never goes into Isaac's closet. Never. I'm the one who dresses him. The one who puts away his toys and packs his diaper bag for school. He never should've found the suitcase. It was hidden. He wouldn't have just stumbled upon it. I was smart about where I'd hid it. Paul goes into every other part of the house, but Isaac's room has always been a place he avoids. Going in there means he'd actually have to dress him or change a diaper or something, and he almost always avoids that. I try to think quickly. "Oh, right, *that* suitcase."

"It's money from your parents, isn't it?"

I blink. So, he doesn't know everything. "Yes," I lie, as his grip gets tighter on my arm. "Just an emergency fund. They keep sending us money, but I know how you feel about using their handouts. I haven't spent a penny of it. I swear."

"But you're keeping it. Why?" He's squeezing my arm so tightly it feels like it'll pop, but I try not to wince. I know from experience any sign of weakness will only make him angrier.

"Just in case. I know how tight things get sometimes. We can get rid of it, if that's what you want. I don't care either way."

His grip lessens slightly, but still, I can't chance pulling away. "Why didn't you tell me about it?"

"I didn't want you to get upset."

He scoffs, tossing my arm back to me with force. "You didn't want me to get upset, so instead, you lied and you hid things from me. And what about the clothes in there for you and Isaac. What am I supposed to think of that?"

"Clothes?" I shake my head. "I have no idea. I don't remember putting clothes in there... Maybe I shoved some in when we moved and forgot about them."

He raises his hand, and I flinch as he grabs a wad of my hair, jerking my face to meet his. "You really must think I'm stupid, don't you?"

"Of course n—" I wince as he tugs harder, standing on my tiptoes to avoid the pain.

"I don't want to be like this, Lessa. Don't you get it? *You* make me this way. I've tried hard, so hard, not to be this person. Not to get mad at you, not to...to..." He can't bring himself to say the words. Can't admit what he does. "I was never this person before. Ask any of my exes. I never laid a hand on them. But you make me this way. You lie and you sneak around and you treat me like garbage. Like you're better than me. Like you'll always be better than me."

"I'm so sorry," I cry. "Please, please just let me throw the money out. Throw the whole bag out, if you want to. It was a mistake. I'm so sorry. I'm so, so sorry."

He shoves my head backward, releasing my hair, and I nearly collapse from the pain. Before I can recover, he's back in my face. This time, he grips my jaw with his thumb and forefinger. "If you ever think about leaving me, I'll kill you. Do you hear me? I am your *husband*. You may not like me, but *you will not embarrass me*. You will not *reject* me. Do you understand?"

"I understand," I whimper. From the table, Isaac begins to cry.

"Now, be a nice little wife and get the baby." He turns and walks away from me, a certain swagger in his walk that wasn't there before.

No matter how he tries to pretend he's changed, I know this is the real him.

Whether or not it's because of me, this is who he's become.

This is whom I will remain married to for the rest of my life.

He disappears down the hallway while I try to calm Isaac, though my hands are shaking so hard I can barely hold him.

THAT NIGHT, after Isaac's asleep, I ease into the bedroom, trying not to wake Paul. Instead, I find him staring at the ceiling with a vacant expression. I brush my teeth and wash my face before changing into my pajamas and slipping into bed next to him.

The suitcase is lying empty on the floor. I don't ask what he's done with the cash or the clothes. It doesn't matter. I'll never see it again, we both know that.

He turns over without a word, and I close my eyes, forcing my breaths to come out slow and even.

Don't let him see your fear.

As I lie in bed, unable to sleep until I hear his snores, I think about my future.

Isaac's future.

A future that doesn't involve Paul.

A future where Paul's dead.

CHAPTER TWENTY-FOUR

BLAKELY

PRESENT DAY

No.

No.

No.

I suck in a sharp breath and regret it instantly. The scent is so powerful it burns my nose, throat, and eyes. My vision blurs, the image in front of me like a mosaic of blood, death, and vomit.

My own vomit.

I can't stop it from rising in my throat then spewing out of my mouth with no warning or control.

There are two women in front of me, their bodies slumped back in office chairs. When I close my eyes, I can still see them. I can't stop myself from looking.

I'd say it's like a car accident I can't look away from, but this is worse. It's not metal I'm staring at—not the crushed bits and pieces of a machine—but rather skin, muscles, bone.

Skull.

Bloody temples, thick with black, dried blood that has oozed down their cheeks, dripped onto their blouses.

Their bodies are bloated and pale, with skin that looks ready to fall off the bone. Like milk that sat too long and developed a film over it.

I'm throwing up again as my vision begins to clear and I see the flies. They swarm in their eyes, noses, mouths, and wounds. White, wiggling maggots are scattered over their bodies like confetti, dropping from their wounds and orifices to the floor as I stare.

Behind me, the front door tears open and Tennessee begins to vomit. He made it outside, at least.

The walls are splattered with blood.

This place looks like a crime scene.

This place is a crime scene.

The thought sends me stumbling back.

My vomit, my DNA is now at the scene of a crime. They'll think I had something to do with this.

It's that thought—not the horrific sight in front of me—that finally sends me darting from the room. I couldn't have been there for more than a minute, but it feels like a lifetime. Like I was born with their rotting faces plastered into my mind and that's how I'll die.

When I close my eyes, when I blink, when I breathe—they're all I can see. I understand the phrase *I can't unsee it* now. It haunts me.

I wish I'd never come here.

That's how it happens, isn't it?

One choice. One seemingly simple decision can change everything. Taking this road instead of that. Going out versus staying in. Accepting an invitation rather than throwing it out. In the blink of an eye, everything can change. For better or for worse.

I nearly trip as I reach the front door, gulping in fresh air. I can't breathe it in fast enough. Tennessee is leaning over the porch railing. He catches my eye over his shoulder and wipes his mouth with the inside of his shirt.

He shakes his head, his skin sallow, eyes haunted. "We have to warn the others."

"We have to catch the police," I whisper. My voice sounds foreign to me, as if it's been years since I've heard it.

Everything is shattered.

Fragmented.

Like no part of my future life will ever be connected to the old life. It's a loss I'd grieve if I had the time or the where-withal. Like the very real losses of my life. But right now, the only thing I know for certain is that something is wrong here. We're in danger. Whoever killed these women could be coming for us next.

Just like that, I start to run.

"How long do you think they've been dead?" Tennessee asks from behind me, trying to keep up. My head spins with panic, bile rising in my throat again.

Blink.

Blood.

Blink.

Maggots.

Blink.

Skull.

Blink.

I could see her skull.

Their skulls.

The way their skin was falling away from their wounds.

I suck in a sharp breath, forcing the thoughts away, but they're back with a vengeance. The images are painful. They burn my mind, my chest, my skin. My fingers hurt, and I clench my fists.

A dull ache forms in my temples.

I may black out again. Maybe I hope I will.

The sky is darker now, though it's not yet dark enough to hide the tears staining my cheeks.

"I'm not sure." A new thought flashes in my mind, something I hadn't realized I'd seen until now. Their name tags:

Nita, Reception; Cindy, Manager.

It's a punch to the gut.

They weren't just bodies. They were people. Real people. With kids, maybe. Or grandkids, even. Somebody must be looking for them. Someone must be worried.

I swallow.

What if no one is? What if they have no one to worry about them? No one to notice that they haven't come home? Nobody to realize they've disappeared?

I try not to think of my own life now, but I can't help it. Who will notice if we disappear today? If none of us make it home alive? How long will it take before I'm missed?

They were just two older women, trying to do their jobs.

What happened to them?

Who did this?

How long had they been there? Waiting for someone to find them? How long did it take for them to die in the first place?

"Do you think...we'll make it in time to catch...the police?" Tennessee asks through ragged breaths.

"We have to." I pick up speed, jogging faster through the forest. It's not an option. I can't bear to think of the alternative. Every few feet, I trip over something—a root or bush—but I can't stop. It's too important.

We aren't safe.

"What...do you think...happened?"

I shake my head, unable to answer. I can't tell him what I think—that they must've been shot. I don't tell him about the way their brains had been splattered across the wall like artwork you might see in an expensive gallery. Brains that, seconds before, might've been thinking about what they'd have for lunch or what show they might catch up on that night.

I feel like I'm going to be sick again. I lick my lips, my throat too dry.

"I keep thinking... What if Cindy wasn't the one who sent those emails? What if whoever did this, whoever's doing this... What if they sent them after they were killed?"

It hadn't occurred to me, but it's not a bad theory. "Yeah, maybe. But why?"

"So no one would...you know, find them, maybe? Maybe the killer is coming back to clean up his mess."

Maybe the killer is coming back for us. No. I force the thought away.

"But then why wouldn't they cancel our reservation? Do you think they just missed one?"

"No idea." He shakes his head, slowing his pace to catch his breath. "I'm hoping the...police will be able to give us answers, but after today, I agree with what...you said earlier. I'm out of here."

I nod, halting in my tracks as the house finally comes into view. I lean over, gripping my knees as my chest rattles with heavy, panicked breaths. "I don't...see any police cars."

"Maybe they haven't made it," he says. "They told us it might be a few hours."

"Yeah, maybe." I swallow, allowing myself a few more seconds of rest before hurrying forward again, Tennessee at my heels. A stitch gnaws at my side, and I force my breath in my nose and out my mouth like I've been taught will ease the pain, but nothing seems to help. "There's something that's bothering me."

"You mean other than the bodies?"

"Yes. Lucy introduced herself as the manager, but Cindy's name tag said *she* was the manager. So, why would Lucy lie? What if she's not even an employee?"

He catches up to me then. "She'd have to be, though, right? How else would...she have known we tried to call? The phone lines were down...so she had to have had a... different way to check the...voice mail. Maybe they have different property managers for...each house and then an overall manager to oversee...everything."

He's probably right, but that does nothing for the unease that has settled into my gut. As we reach the house and climb the stairs, I notice the cars are all gone, so the tow truck, at least, has been here. But what about the police?

Please, please don't let us have missed the police.

We walk in the house to both total silence and utter chaos. The breath I'm still trying to control is ripped from my lungs.

"Holy shit. What happened here?" Tennessee asks, eyes wide as he takes in the scene. The room has been torn apart. There are papers, kitchen utensils, and home decor strewn everywhere. The kitchen chairs are knocked over, food scattered on the floor. I pick up a throw pillow and place it on the kitchen island as I walk past the hall, like that'll somehow help the disaster in front of me.

"Hello? Anyone here?" This feels like the moment the girl walks into the basement in a horror movie. Every part of me wants to run, but where? Where can I go? We have no phones, no cars, and no place to hide.

"Where did they go?" he asks, setting up a candle that was knocked over on the tabletop.

I shake my head. "We should check our rooms."

In truth, I'm scared of what we'll find. Scared they'll be there and dead. That we're too late. I'm not sure I can stomach seeing another dead body today...or ever, for that matter. I don't need to say we'll stick together for him to wait for me. It's clear now, we're in this together, like it or not. If there's one person I trust in the house, it's Tennessee, though just days ago, he would've been my last choice.

We ease down the hall and he shoves open his bedroom door. It hits the wall behind it with a loud thud. "What the hell?" He darts across the room, taking in the scene. His suitcase and bags have been dumped out on the bed, his clothes and toiletries thrown everywhere.

He opens his laptop bag, staring into it, then looks around with wide eyes and a slack jaw. "Someone took my laptop."

"What? No."

"I put it back in here after I messaged my mom. It's..."
He shoves a hand inside the black bag. "It's gone."

I dash out of his room, headed for mine.

No.

No.

No.

Please no.

I don't have much, but it's all I have.

The story I'm working on is all I have left. If someone
has stolen it...

I jog down the stairs and push open my door to find my
room in the same state of disarray. I rush to the bed, throwing
the covers all about, confirming what I already know.

It's gone.

My laptop.

My life's work.

It's gone.

I turn around, rage blurring my vision, and shake my
head as Tennessee rubs a hand through his hair. I check the
door to my patio, just to be sure, but it's still locked, just as
I've kept it. "I don't understand. Would the police have done
this?"

"Stolen our stuff and trashed our house? No, I wouldn't
think so." Panic swells in my stomach. None of this makes
any sense. A dull throb begins in my temple, and I reach for
my pain pills as Tennessee turns away from me. I slip three
into my mouth and swallow them dry, listening as he knocks
on Lyra's door.

"Lyra, you in there?"

I join him in the hall seconds before he pushes it open.
Sure enough, her room is just as messy as the rest of the

house, and there's no laptop to be found. We rush upstairs, praying to be proven wrong as we check Aidy's and Dan's bedrooms.

"What happened here? It...it looks like there was a struggle. Or...a robbery. But where is everyone?" When Tennessee speaks again, his words send chills down my spine. "Maybe someone took our stuff and took them, too."

The killer.

Something splinters in my chest, the amount of panic I feel indescribable. We're too late. We didn't make it in time. We couldn't save them.

They'll be coming for us next.

Lightning cracks overhead as finally the rain sets in, hail pounding the metal roof of the house. The sound assaults my ears, my senses heightened.

"We need to think. We have to get out of here and get help. If the police came, whoever did this must've come after." Not the killer. Anyone but the killer. I can't say the words aloud. Can't allow myself to think them anymore.

"Unless they came before and then, when the police came, there was no one to answer the door."

"Unless the police are involved." I huff. "I thought you said this town was a safe place."

"I thought it was," he says with a sigh. "Look, we can't go anywhere in this storm. Let's go downstairs and do what we can to barricade the house. Whatever's going on, we're going to have to ride out the storm, and then, first thing in the morning, we'll go for help."

"Are you crazy? We can't stay here!"

I can't keep the thoughts at bay any longer.

Killer.

Killer.

There's a killer on the loose, and they're coming for us.

"What choice do we have? The storm is too bad. It's already dark out. We're surrounded by woods, and god knows what animals are out there after dark. We can't make it to town in these conditions. I'm not saying we let our guard down, okay? I'm saying we sit down, take a breath, gather some weapons and supplies, and prepare to get help as soon as morning comes."

My headache seems to dull at his words, my rational mind taking over. As much as I hate to admit it, he's right. We both know it's not safe to travel the woods at this time of night, especially with this storm raging. We have no idea who's out there, who did this, where the others are, or what's going on. I squeeze my eyes shut. "Okay, fine. You're right. We have to be smart about this."

"Hey, if there's anyone who can figure this out, it's us. We do this stuff every day." He smirks, trying to lighten the mood.

I move past him and down the stairs. "Yeah, well, I may have to change careers after this." He doesn't know I'm not joking.

The lightning cracks again, and then, as if to further make things worse, the lights flicker and we're plunged into total darkness.

CHAPTER TWENTY-FIVE

LESSA

BEFORE

He hit me again.

Still not a punch—*never* a punch—it was only a slap. I don't know why that matters, but it does. Somewhere, a part of my mind still tries to rationalize it. I tell myself it's not abuse if he doesn't leave a bruise, if he doesn't punch me with his fist, if he doesn't break the skin or make me bleed, if he apologizes after.

I tell myself I'm not *that* girl.

That this isn't real.

That he won't do it again.

That I should be able to stop it somehow.

That other people have it worse.

Still, as I stare at the red handprint across my shoulder in the mirror, I find myself playing out a scenario that's been in my head for the past few weeks.

There's no going back from this, my rational self warns the feral animal who's been backed into a corner.

If you kill him, you'll go to prison. You'll never be the same. You'll never see your son.

If I don't, he'll kill me.

Today, it was because he said I'd dared to *talk back* when he told me Isaac needed his diaper changed. I was in the middle of preparing dinner when he shouted it from the living room. I hadn't thought; I just responded.

It was simple—not even meant to be rude.

"So, change him."

But that was enough.

It was enough to set him off and give him a reason to remind me of all that he was.

"Don't I do enough around here?" he'd bellowed as he slammed his hand into my back, knocking me down and sending pasta sauce flying across the room. "Working all day to give you this nice house isn't enough?"

At this point, I don't think he's talking to me when he says these things. I think, in his mind, he'll never be enough for me. That's what it all comes down to, and that's what pisses him off and terrifies me.

I pull my shirt back up, covering his handprint, and stare into the mirror.

Can I really do this?

What is the alternative?

Do I want Isaac to grow up thinking this is normal?

Can I go back to my parents and tell them what's happening? Would they help me?

No. I made this mess myself and, if I'm ever going to get out from under my family's wing, I have to deal with it myself too. I have to grow up. Otherwise, I'll just be letting someone else control me.

I never want to be controlled again.

I shut off the light, unable to look at myself anymore as I step out into the hall.

My thoughts rage.

There's no going back from this.

You're about to kill someone.

You'll be a murderer.

You don't have to do this.

Louder than all the voices is the voice telling me if I don't do this, this will be my existence forever. Cowering on the kitchen floor, waiting for the next blow. Examining wounds in the bathroom mirror. Praying Isaac isn't old enough to be scared by this yet.

This will be my existence until he kills me, either by accident or on purpose.

In the bedroom, Paul is asleep under the covers. I cross the room quietly and ease open the top dresser drawer. With shaking hands, I pull out the handgun his grandfather gave him for Christmas when he was fifteen.

Paul showed me how to turn the safety on and off once, though he never got around to showing me how to check whether it's loaded. I weigh it in my hands... Isn't that how you're supposed to tell? I have no idea what I'm feeling for exactly, or how heavy it should be.

This is ridiculous. What am I doing?

"What are you doing?"

I jump at the sound of his voice echoing my own thoughts. He's right behind me and he lunges for me, but I'm quicker. I dart from the room and down the hall, slamming into the wall as I stumble over my own feet. Paul's still right behind me. He grabs at my hair and narrowly misses. In the kitchen, I turn to face him, my chest rising and falling with erratic breaths. My hands shake so much it's impossible to hold the gun steady as I lift it.

He sneers at me. "What are you doing with that thing? You look ridiculous."

"I want to...leave, Paul. Me and Isaac. We're going to...go a-and you're going to let us."

"Like hell." He steps forward, holding out a hand. "Give me that before you hurt yourself. Is this about earlier? That was nothing. Just a love tap, really. I was just in a bad mood. You know I didn't mean it."

I step back so he can't reach for the gun. "I don't love you anymore. I don't want to be with you. I want you to leave. You will never hurt me again."

His eyes darken, his jaw tightening. He glances toward the hallway, and I see it in his eyes as soon as he realizes it. He's closer to Isaac's bedroom than I am. If he wants to, he can get to him first. He can scoop him from his crib. Hurt him. Kill him.

Would he?

I don't know.

I don't have time to contemplate. To think.

I don't have time.

He turns to run, to dart for him, to do god knows what to our child, and I pull the trigger.

Bang.

The shot misses, but it's enough to scare him. He stumbles and grabs for the kitchen table. Because it's a pedestal

173

table, his weight causes it to flip. It crashes to the ground as I fire again.

This time, I'm close enough that I don't miss.

This time, the bullet connects with his chest.

A bloom of red spreads over his white T-shirt.

I don't feel it.

I feel nothing.

Something inside of me has flipped off.

I'm totally and completely numb.

I watch him bleed out on the floor. It only takes seconds. He doesn't beg for his life—he's too proud for that. Instead, he just stares at me and smiles.

I'm free, I think. *I'm finally free.*

As he takes his last breath, I wonder if that's how he feels too.

CHAPTER TWENTY-SIX

BLAKELY

PRESENT DAY

"We'll take turns staying awake," Tennessee says. In the grand scheme of things, maybe it's not a bad plan, but the idea that I could ever sleep in this house, ever sleep again for that matter, is laughable. "One of us can keep watch while the other rests, and then we'll swap." He seems to read my expression, because he adds, "I know. I don't think I could possibly fall asleep right now, but maybe eventually. For now, we can just sit up and talk until the power comes back on."

The front door slams open, and we both jolt.

Someone tries to flick the light on.

"What the hell?"

"Lyra?" I shoot up at the sound of her voice. "Oh my god, is that you?"

"Who the hell else would it be? Why are y'all sitting around here in the dark like some kind of vampires?" I hear the clang of silverware as someone steps on the proof that this afternoon actually happened.

"Power's out," Tennessee says. He lifts the candle we found into the air. "Because of the storm. Watch your step. This place is a mess."

"I can...sort of see that. What happened?"

"Where have you guys been?" I ask, trying to make out their faces in the darkness. "We thought something happened to you."

"We went to the police station," Aidy says. "They had us come down and file a report."

"How did you get back?" I hurry past them, clinging to a tiny thread of hope. "Did someone bring you?"

"Officer Greenly brought us back once we'd talked to the detectives," Aidy says, spinning to watch me run out the door. "Why?"

"Don't let him leave!" Tennessee shouts, darting after me.

"He's already gone," Lyra says. "Will someone tell us what is going on here?"

"Is something wrong?" Aidy asks.

Out the door, refusing to give up, I dart down the stairs and run the length of the steep driveway, my shoes skidding along the gravel. Rain pelts my skin, soaking through my clothes and pasting my hair to my face and neck.

Desperate to see the red glow of taillights, to hear the faint hum of a car's engine, I picture them seeing me in their rearview, stopping to see what's wrong. Wrapping me in one of those blankets you see on TV to keep me from going into shock or whatever.

How does one know if you're going into shock, by the way? You'd think I'd know this.

My feet pound on the pavement as I reach it, searching the darkness for any piece of hope. They can't have gone far. This can't be over. When my legs and lungs burn for relief, I stop, leaning forward to catch my breath.

They're gone.

It's over.

My last piece of hope evaporates in seconds.

I blink into the darkness, praying, praying, praying for a sign of life somewhere. A sign that we aren't alone. But it doesn't come.

I stand up and turn around, blinking rain from my eyes. I can see Tennessee's candle on the porch, retreating back into the house, and I follow. At this point, all I can hope for is that Lyra and Aidy will have a way to reach the police. A way to bring them back to us. I jog back up the stairs, my legs so sore they feel bruised, and step into the blackness of the house.

I do my best to wipe the cool rain from my skin, but it does little to prevent the chill in the air from causing me to shiver.

The candle Tennessee is holding illuminates the space only slightly. He's not looking at me. "What, um, what did they say?"

"The police? Well, they don't seem optimistic that they'll find our stuff," Aidy says. "But they took our statement and said they'll try to contact the property manager to see if someone may have access to the house."

"Speaking of, did you guys find the office? You were gone forever," Lyra says.

Tennessee and I exchange a look. "We found it," he says finally. "But...the reason Blakely just tried to stop the police from leaving is because we also found two bodies there. Office workers, we think. We aren't sure how long they've been dead."

"What?" Aidy gasps.

"You serious?" Lyra asks.

"Does it sound like we're joking?" Tennessee's tone is sharp.

"I'm processing, okay? Are we talking dead, as in natural causes, or..."

"We need to get out of here," I say. "If what we saw is any indication, we're in danger. We need to leave. Or call for help. Wait a second..." I pause. "Where's Daniel?"

Tennessee lifts the candle, tilting it forward to get a better look around our circle.

"You mean he's not here?" Aidy asks.

"No. When we got back, you were all gone," I say.

"Wait, *what?*" Lyra asks. "No. We left him here. He was supposed to be here to tell you guys where we went."

"Well, he's not," Tennessee tells them. "We looked everywhere."

"Oh my god, did they get him?" Aidy cries. "This can't be happening."

"Are you sure the people were dead? I mean, could it have just been some sort of Halloween decoration?" Lyra asks skeptically.

Maggots.

Blood.

Bone.

"It wasn't a decoration." I'm not going to defend my memory or my ability to distinguish a murder scene from a bit of Halloween fun. "We need to get help. And find Daniel."

"Did you guys get phones while you were in town?" Tennessee moves the candle so he can see their hands. "She's right. We need to call the police."

"No, we didn't." Lyra flashes her empty palms. "We're leaving in the morning. As soon as the tow guy drops Aidy's car off, we're going to the airport. I'll get a new phone when I land. No sense getting one here if it'll just disappear again."

I can't see her face, but I hear the accusation in her tone and choose to ignore it. Right now, it's the least of my concerns.

There is a killer on the loose—potentially coming after us —someone in our group is missing, and we're standing around talking like it's no big deal.

Why isn't anyone else freaking out?

"He's going to be okay, right?" Aidy's voice is soft. "I mean, he can't be... How could he just disappear?"

I flash back to the mess in the house. *It looks like there was a struggle here,* Tennessee had said. What if that struggle was Daniel fighting for his life?

I can't bear to think about it.

Can't handle the weight that comes with knowing I may be responsible for something happening to him. We should've never split up.

"*Speaking of disappearing,*" Tennessee says, drawing the words out, "I guess we should tell you that all of our laptops are missing now, too."

"Wait, what?"

"You're kidding, right?"

Their responses come at once, panic filled and furious.

As if this has really allowed the gravity of the situation to set in.

"He's not kidding. We came home and the house had been ransacked. All of our stuff has been torn through, and we couldn't find anyone's laptops, unless you've hidden them somewhere we wouldn't think to look."

"Wait, wait, wait. You honestly expect us to believe you two are just innocent little bystanders, stumbling onto a crime scene? You left, alone, and just happened to find two dead bodies that you have no proof of? And someone conveniently came into the house *after* we left but *before* you came home and no one saw them? Really?" Lyra clicks her tongue.

"What did you want me to do?" I demand. "Take a fucking picture?"

"No, I've had you pegged right from the start. Come in here with your whole, 'oh, I'm your biggest fan' spiel, but as soon as my notes went missing, I understood what you were playing at. And Tennessee is all too happy to follow you around like a lost puppy if it means you'll show him any attention. I see your game, Blakely."

"And what's that?" I demand. "I didn't take your freaking notes, okay? I wasn't in your room, and I certainly didn't take your laptop. This isn't a game or a joke or anything else. This is serious. We're in dang—"

"No. You're just jealous because I beat you out for an Edgar last year. You thought I didn't remember that, but I do. This is all some little ploy to throw me off my game—"

Rage bubbles in my belly, making me feel ill. "Wow, you really are full of yourself, aren't you? You think I invited everyone here just to steal your story because you beat me out for some award? Really? We don't even write in the same genre. What use would I have for your story?"

"Nothing, other than making sure I can't write it. People've done worse. We all heard the stories last year about people drugging drinks at the Southern Writers Convention. In fact, as I recall, you were the only speaker who didn't make a complete fool of yourself that night. Convenient, wasn't it?"

"You have no idea what you're talking about!" I shout, my head growing fuzzy. I rub my temples. She's not wrong. I do recall hearing those rumors, but they were just stupid, unfounded rumors. Nothing was ever proven and, at that point, the convention and publishing world drama were the last things on my mind.

"Guys, please!" Aidy begs. "Can we not fight? This is bad enough. *Daniel is missing.* We need to do something! We can't just stand here."

"Sure. Tell Bonnie and Clyde here to give us back our laptops, 'fess up to lying about the dead bodies, tell us where Daniel is, and we'll forget this ever happened," Lyra snaps.

"We didn't take them, we're not lying, and we have no idea where he is," Tennessee says through gritted teeth. "This isn't about Blakely and me. It's all of us together. We can't do this right now. We have to figure out how to get out of here alive." I hardly hear him. My head is fuzzy, and I can no longer feel my feet.

No.

Please, no.

Then, the darkness comes again.

CHAPTER TWENTY-SEVEN

When I wake, the first thing I notice is Tennessee's scent. I didn't even realize I knew it, but there it is. Clean, like soap, with a hint of mint toothpaste and leather.

I open my eyes, but they don't seem open because I see nothing.

I stir, sitting up and patting them.

Oh, god, no. I've lost my sight. I've lost my—

"You okay?"

His voice is low and calm. It brings me back to reality, and I remember the power outage.

"Why's it so dark? Where's the candle?"

"I dropped it when I realized you were falling, and it went out. Lyra's looking for another match."

In the distance, Lyra groans. "They really oughta have flashlights around here somewhere."

"There may've been one under my bathroom sink," Aidy says, and I hear her moving away from us.

"How long was I out?" I ask as Tennessee helps me to sit up.

"Just a few seconds. A minute at most. You...you okay?"

I nod, though he can't see me. "I will be. Just..."

"Stress, right. I know. I think we're all pretty stressed right now."

I pull my knees into my chest, squeezing my arms around them as tears form in my eyes. I've never been so thankful for the darkness. "I have to find my laptop," I whisper.

"I know. We'll find them. Did you have your story backed up?"

"No." I squeeze my eyes shut, knowing damn well this is no one's fault but my own. How many times have I heard horror stories about lost manuscripts? I knew how important this one was. I knew what it meant, and I took no precautions.

I feel the weight of my answer in his exhale. "That's rough. Mine's backed up, but the thought of someone having access to it right now terrifies me. Just...try not to stress over it, okay? We'll get out of here, get somewhere safe, go to the police to report the murders, and then you'll be able to focus on your rewrite. The bright side is that's the least of our problems, right?"

"I don't have time for a rewrite," I tell him, blinking back tears.

"Deadline's looming?" His tone is clipped and disinterested. I know he feels like I'm being unreasonable.

"Yeah. Something like tha—"

"Here we go!" Lyra cries. "Matches."

In seconds, she's close to us again, and we listen as she

fumbles to find the candle and light it. When she does, I take in the sight of each of our faces. We're huddled on the floor of the living room, all looking more than a bit frightened.

"Why are you crying?" Lyra asks, her eyes narrowing in on me.

I shake my head, drying my cheeks with the collar of my shirt. "I'm fine. Just nerves."

"Okay, well, I need to go check on Aidy. I'm taking the candle. Will you guys be okay here?"

Whatever fight we were having, at least for the moment, it seems to be forgotten.

"Yep." I nod, and she looks to Tennessee, who agrees before she stands with the candle and makes her way down the hall.

When we're alone, I hear Tennessee's voice again. "Are you sure you're okay?"

I open my mouth to answer, but nothing comes out. I feel a cautious hand slip around my shoulders and, comforted by his scent, I let my head find solace in the crook of his neck. A tear slips down my cheek and I brush it away, sniffling.

"Hey, so, you're still protecting me, right?" He chuckles under his breath.

Recalling our conversation earlier, I laugh. "Yep, I've got your back."

He nods, his cheek rubbing against my head. "Good. Well, I know you don't need it, but for the record, I've got yours too."

More tears fall, and we sit there silently. He doesn't ask any further questions, doesn't push me for answers, just sits while I cry on his shoulder.

"Aidy?" Lyra's voice echoes down the hall.

A bedroom door shuts, the faint light of her candle disappearing.

"So, what's your story about?" Tennessee asks, obviously trying to distract me.

"I don't really know yet."

"What?" He pulls away slightly.

"I'm struggling with it. Originally, it was about a missing child."

"Wouldn't that be hard after..."

"I thought it would be a good way to work through losing my son, but it was so much harder than I expected. Writing has always been like therapy for me, but it was too soon. I wasn't ready."

"I don't blame you for that. I... I still have trouble writing about father-son relationships, and I lost mine years and years ago. It's just too hard."

I press my lips together. "I just want to make sure this book means something."

"I get that for sure. The constant pressure for each book to be better than your last."

"Right." I drag in a long inhale. "But it's more than that..."

"How so?"

"This book is going to be my last."

He's quiet for a moment and, when he speaks again, his tone is cautious. "Are you...retiring?"

"Something like that."

"Because of what happened to your family?"

"No," I say quickly, though I guess it's not entirely true. "It's just time."

Before he can say anything else, a noise from upstairs

draws our attention. I suck in a sharp breath. "Who's upstairs?"

"Dan's room's the only one up there."

"*Daniel?*" I shout.

We're both on our feet in an instant, feeling for the staircase. We ease our way up each step, and at one point, Tennessee holds out his hand to steady me. "Careful."

I follow his lead, one easy step at a time, keeping one hand gripped firmly on the banister and the other in his palm. Once we reach the top floor, Tennessee releases my hand. "Wait here."

I listen to the sounds of him finding his way across the room, the sweeping noise of his palm against the wall, the bump of his shoe as it hits a table. Finally, I hear him knock on Dan's door. "Daniel, you in there?"

Click.

The door opens.

"Daniel?" he calls again. Then, "No answer."

I release a breath. "I'm sure I heard something up here."

"The darkness has us all messed up. It was probably Aidy and Lyra." His hands find me again in the darkness. "Come on, let's go back downstairs and see if they managed to find flashlights."

He leads me to the staircase, and we descend the same way we climbed. Once safely on the bottom floor, he calls out, "Lyra? Aidy? Did you find anything?"

We're met with only silence. I feel him tense next to me.

"Aidy?" I call.

Down the hall, I hear a sound I don't recognize right away.

"Is that..."

"A shower?" Tennessee fills in. "Yeah, I think so."

We feel our way down the hallway, more confused than anything, and knock on the bathroom door. "Hello? Lyra? Aidy? Are you guys in there?"

In an instant, the shower shuts off.

"Lyra?" I'm getting impatient. Why isn't she answering? "Is everything okay?" I reach for the handle. "I'm coming in, okay? Are you dressed?"

"Are you sick?" Tennessee asks.

When we don't get a response, I twist the handle and push the door open.

The room is dark, but I can see a hint of light coming from the cracked open doorway leading to Aidy's bedroom.

"Lyra?"

I step forward cautiously and pull it open.

The single candle rests on the nightstand, illuminating the bedroom only slightly. It gives us just enough light to see that, somehow, the room is completely empty.

They've both vanished.

Tennessee's quiet question comes slowly, confirming this is real. "Where did they go?"

CHAPTER TWENTY-EIGHT

"Okay, okay, let's, um, let's be rational about this..." Tennessee says, following behind me as I rush out of the bathroom and down the hall toward the kitchen. "I mean, they couldn't have gone far, right? They have to be around here. Maybe they're upstairs, after all."

"Tennessee, we saw them both go down the hall, and now they're not there. They disappeared, just like Daniel. Just like our stuff."

"But...but, I mean, that's not possible."

"Apparently it *is*. Now, I know earlier we agreed that staying here might be the safest thing, but right now, we're being picked off one by one. By whom, I don't know. Your ghost, maybe? An old tenant, more likely? Who knows? Maybe the maintenance team is exacting revenge for unfair working conditions. I've watched enough of the ID Channel that I know nothing's impossible. But whatever is going on here, I don't want to stick around and be next. We have to get out of here, and I truly think we're no safer in this house than we would be out there. The storm is dying down..." I glance toward the front door, hoping it's true. We can't see anything, but I can no longer hear the rain pelting the roof. "I say we make a run for it."

"I'm not saying it's a terrible idea, I just—" He cuts off, and my heart lurches. Did he disappear, too?

No, stop that.

"Tennessee?"

A hand touches my shoulder, and he spins me around, toward the large picture windows in the living room. "Look." His voice is a breathless whisper in my ear.

It takes me just seconds to discover what it is he wants me to look at. In the distance, beyond the glass of the windows, I see it.

A flashlight.

Someone's moving around outside the house. We're staring at nearly the same spot we were the first night when we saw the light outside the window. I'd nearly forgotten about it with so much else going on.

"Let's go." I start to move, but he grabs my arm.

"Wait."

I feel him move away from me and hear him fumbling in the kitchen. He bumps into the island. Seconds later, a drawer slides open.

"Knives?" I guess.

The drawer shuts, and I hold my breath.

"Be still," he warns, seconds before his hand connects with my skin. He turns my hand over and places a knife handle in my palm. "Here you go. Just...just in case."

I grip the handle, turning my attention back to the

window. Together, we cross the room and search for the side door that leads out to the patio where the hot tub is.

He eases the sliding glass door open slowly, trying to minimize the noise it makes, but it's no use. The door groans against the rusty metal track. I shoot a glance toward the flashlight in the distance.

Crack.

We duck for cover, hitting the floor as a noise fills the air.

"Was that?" I ask breathlessly, running a hand over my hair to make sure I'm all in one piece.

"Yeah," Tennessee confirms. "It was a gunshot."

I look out into the woods, my heart thudding in my ears. "Tennessee, look!" The flashlight has fallen to the ground, the light casting shadows all around.

I feel along the ground for the knife and pick it up when my fingers connect with the metal. Tennessee grips me under my arm, helping me to my feet, and we move forward.

The light is coming from far away and, as we get closer, I have a vague suspicion about where it is. It's confirmed when we begin to climb the hill we hiked earlier this morning.

"The bunker," I tell him as we draw nearer.

"I thought so, too." He slows his pace a bit so I can catch up.

When we're nearly there, I catch sight of something on the ground near the flashlight. A boulder sinks in my core. "What the..."

I drop my knife, darting forward and dropping to the ground.

No. No. No. No. No.

Tennessee sinks down next to me, and finally, I can see his face and the horror written across it.

I brush Aidy's hair out of her face with shaking hands, searching for a pulse. I can't feel anything. My fingers are practically numb from the chill in the air and the pure shock I'm feeling.

This can't be happening.

It can't.

We can't lose anyone else.

"Aidy?" It's not possible. *She can't be...* My hands connect with a wetness on her stomach. Her shirt is drenched in blood. I snatch the flashlight from the ground, nearly too scared to confirm my suspicions.

"Was she shot?" Tennessee asks.

I nod, biting down on my lower lip in hopes the pain will keep me conscious. The flashlight beam connects with the bullet wound, and I gasp, dropping the flashlight and smacking my hands over the wound to apply pressure. "Give me your jacket."

He does as he's told, handing over his jacket and using it to cover her wound.

"We have to get her out of here. We have to get help or she's... She's not going to make it. She has to make it."

"Can we get her in the house? Me and you? Do you think you can help me carry her?"

I nod, chewing my bottom lip. "We have to try."

Bang.

I flinch as another gunshot tears through the night.

"That came from inside the house," Tennessee says, standing to his feet and brushing off his knees. "I have to go back. Someone else could be hurt. Can you stay with her?"

"What? *No!* You can't leave me out here alone."

"Well, we can't leave her and we can't bring her back to the house right now. We don't have the time."

I race through our options in my head. Whom can we save? Whom should we save? What should we do?

"Help!" a voice in the distance cries, interrupting my thoughts.

I stand up, shining the flashlight in the direction of the voice. It's not one I recognize. "Did you..."

"Hear that," he confirms. "Who's there?"

"Please help..." The voice is soft and weak. In pain, maybe.

Tennessee looks my way. "I'll go. You stay here with Aidy. If anything happens to me, you run as far and as fast as you can and get help."

"I told you, in my books, we don't let the men save the day." I shake my head. "I'm coming with you. Just give me a second." I bend down, wrapping his jacket around Aidy in an attempt to make a tourniquet. "I'm so sorry," I whisper, though I know she can't hear me. "I'll be back." I stand, trying to fight against the guilt weighing on my mind as we move in the direction the sound came from.

"Can you hear us?" he cries out. "Tell us where you are, and we'll come to you."

"Please... Please help me."

I stop in my tracks, reaching out to grab his arm. "Wait. What if this is a trap?"

He's still for a moment. "What should we do?"

I wave the light in the general direction of the voice. "Come out where we can see you!"

I hold my breath as Tennessee's hand slips down into mine and we hang on to each other for dear life. A few seconds later, a figure emerges from the edge of the woods near the driveway. A figure covered in blood.

My heart races in my chest as I recognize her. *"Lucy?"* I shout, dropping Tennessee's hand and racing forward. She looks so frail, hobbling along the path to us. "Oh, God. Tennessee, she was shot!" I reach the woman's side quickly, taking in the sight of her injuries.

She stands in front of me in what looks like shock. Blood has drenched her right arm, and she's using her hand to try to stop the bleeding as she looks up at me with haunted, blood-shot eyes. "I... He came out of nowhere."

"Who?" Tennessee demands. "Who came out of nowhere?"

"Why are you here, Lucy?"

"Heard the...gunshots. I just live...*thatta way.*" She points aimlessly. "Thought I could help."

"Where? Close enough we could walk? Could we use your phone to call for help?" I ask, practically begging.

"Who shot you, Lucy? Did you get a good look at him? Did you see which direction he went?" Tennessee is in her face now, dismissing my questions to ask his own. His words are firm and pointed.

"Thatta way..." she whispers, turning her attention back to her arm. "I think it's really bad."

"Do you have a cell phone, Lucy?" I lower my face so I'm eye level with her, speaking slowly. "Or a house phone we could use?"

"It's...um..." She blinks slowly and staggers, a hand to her head.

I grip her unwounded arm, trying to steady her. "It's

going to be okay." I shrug off my sweater and do my best to tighten it around the wound, trying to think.

My brain is muddled with panic and stress, still fighting against my new reality.

But this is our reality.

I have to make a decision, no matter how much I don't like it. We have no idea how far away Lucy's home is, or if we'll be able to make it there to call for help.

All I know for sure is that if we keep standing here, she's going to bleed out. "Okay, here's what we're going to do. Can you hear me, Lucy? Can you focus? Let's get you inside so I can get you bandaged up and then we can try to get to your phone and call for help. Just breathe, okay? It's going to be alright."

"Mercy...mercy me. You're so...so kind, my dear." Her words have begun to slur, her voice soft and watery. I'm afraid I'm going to lose her if we don't act quickly. My mind flicks to Aidy, still alone and lying in the grass, but I force the thought away. I can only help one person at a time, and Lucy is still conscious. She has to be my priority.

Inside, I pass the flashlight to Tennessee. "Hold this."

I work quickly to remove my sweater from her arm. "I'm going to have to take your arm out of your sleeve, Lucy, okay? I have to see where the blood is coming from."

"He came out of nowhere..."

She answers a question I didn't ask, and I cast a glance over my shoulder at Tennessee. We're running out of time. She's lost so much blood.

"Did you know him, Lucy? Was he tall with dark brown, kind of wavy hair, and a beard?"

He's describing Daniel.

"He was... He was..." Her face goes slack, then she meets my eyes again. "I heard the gunshot. I just wanted to help."

"I know, Lucy, I know. I'm going to help you now, okay?" I ease her arm out of the sleeve, moving my fingers across her wrinkled skin. I use my sweater to wipe away some of the blood, searching for the wound, but I can't find it.

I lift her arm farther, checking her sides, then her back.

But there's nothing.

It's as if she's not bleeding from her arm at all.

I turn my attention to her arm again, trying to find the wound in the shadows from the flashlight. "Can you move this way some, Tennessee? I can't see... I can't find the wound."

"What?" He steps closer, helping me search.

"Hey, what's..." My eyes fall to the waistband of her pants, where a black handgun rests. I shoot a petrified glance up at her, meeting her wry grin with panic.

No.

"Lucy, why do you have that?" I ask, already knowing the answer.

She covers her mouth with a bloody hand. "Oopsie."

CHAPTER TWENTY-NINE

Before I can comprehend what's happening, Tennessee grabs my arm and shoves me forward, past Lucy and toward the hall. I nearly drop the flashlight, but I manage to hang on to it as a gunshot tears through the house. We duck as I shriek, and he pushes me to run faster.

Lucy the property manager is shooting into the dark at us, and I'm running through the house with Tennessee Rivers. My life has become a mystery novel, and nothing about it makes any sense at the moment.

I'm starting to wonder if this is all a hallucination.

He shoves us into his bedroom and slams the door shut, pushing me out of the way just in time for another shot to ring out.

I whimper, clinging to a bedpost as my mind races to try to piece together my new reality.

His hands cup my face. "Are you okay? Are you blacking out?"

"I'm okay," I whisper. "Though I don't know how. You saved me. I froze, and you... Thank you."

"You're welcome. Now, come on. We need to barricade the door."

"Knock, knock." Lucy's soft voice is right outside the door. She twists the handle, but it's locked. Tennessee shoves a dresser across the floor, and I stand to help him. We use all of our strength to move the two dressers in the room in front of the door, and finally, he points to the armoire. "Let's get this next. We can lay it across them."

I move to one side of the armoire, preparing myself, and he follows my lead, reaching over me. "On the count of three."

I nod as he counts, and on three, we shove with all our might.

When we do, cool air hits me. I jerk back. "What the..."

I turn to see the source of the air and find myself staring at a doorway that had been hidden behind the armoire. Glancing at Tennessee, who appears equally confused from what I can see, I reach for the flashlight on the bed.

"What is this?" he asks.

The second I grab hold of the flashlight, I spin around, pointing it at the door. The door swings open, and I gasp.

Two hands shoot out, grabbing us and jerking us into the darkness before we have time to scream.

CHAPTER THIRTY

When I try to scream, a hand clamps over my mouth. The taste of her scented lotion burns my tongue.

"*Shut up!*"

I recognize the voice and blink as her face comes into focus. "Lyra?"

"Yeah, it's me, now shut up before you get us all killed." She grabs our hands and drags us farther into the shadowy room.

"Where are you taking us?" Tennessee asks.

"Somewhere a hell of a lot better than where you're coming from."

When she stops, I'm not exactly sure she's right. The room is small and damp smelling. Musty. The light from our flashlight does little to illuminate the space, but it's enough. There are rafters above our heads and the walls are all studs, plywood, and insulation.

"Is this...an attic?"

"Not exactly, no. We're, for lack of a better explanation,

in the walls, I guess," Lyra says. "Or...a section of them, anyway. I haven't been able to figure out how far they go."

"How did you find this place?"

"When I went into Aidy's room earlier, the big armoire thing was standing open and I could see a cutout in the back. Some *Chronicles of Narnia* shit."

"So, you just...what? Just went in it?" Tennessee asks.

"I wasn't exactly feeling any safer out there with you two," she snips. "And anyway, what I think you mean to say is *thank you*, because I just saved your asses. I stepped inside, and I realized I could hear you guys. I walked all down this way." She points down a long, narrow space. "It leads upstairs."

"So, that's what we heard." I gasp.

"And then, I came back this way because I heard a gunshot. I could hear you guys running, and it sounded like you were right outside this door, so I opened it to help you and...you'd found me."

"All the armoires have doors behind them, then?" Tennessee asks. "In the backs?"

Lyra shrugs. "I guess so. These are the only doors I've found so far, but these walls and stairs go on for a while. You could probably circle the whole house within the walls."

He scratches his head. "But...how? How is this here? And...and why?"

"I don't know. From what I can tell, it looks like there are tunnels and doorways going to every one of the rooms in the house. They're probably all hidden behind some sort of furniture. It would explain how someone was getting around."

"And how they were taking our things." I shiver.

"So, someone was moving around in the walls this whole time? In our bedrooms? Listening to us?" Tennessee asks. "Who would do that?"

"Lucy," I say softly.

"What?" They both turn to me.

"Why?" Tennessee asks. "Why would she do this to us? Do you know her? Does she have some grudge against you?"

"No, but I think I know who she is. When I first met her, I thought she looked familiar, but I couldn't figure out why. I think she's Lessa Astor."

"Who?" Lyra demands.

"The woman who used to live here. The one who's been missing. The one whose husband was murdered in this house. I'd been reading an article about it the day we met. The photograph of her was from thirty, forty years ago, at least, but...today it clicked."

"And you're sure that's who it is?" Tennessee asks cautiously.

"I'm not positive, no, but it's a guess. She's obviously the one behind all of this. Wouldn't it make sense if she's somehow been here all along?"

"But why? She's gotta be, like, sixty at this point, right? Why would she want to hurt us? And, more importantly, how? How is she getting around and accomplishing all of this without getting caught?" Tennessee's question hangs in the air.

"Maybe someone's been helping her," Lyra suggests. "From the inside."

A quiet giggle fills the space, and I turn toward it, aiming the flashlight until the beam lands down a hallway to our right, where Lucy is emerging from the shadows.

A confirmation fills my chest. I was right.

Tennessee takes a protective step toward me. "*Why* are you doing this?"

She laughs. "Well, why don't we ask her, since she's got it all figured out?"

"It was you, wasn't it? You're Lessa?" I demand.

"Once upon a time I was. No one's called me that in years," she says simply.

"You're supposed to be missing."

"Well, here I am." Her hands rise in a shrug. "Found me."

"What happened that night? Did someone take you and your son or..." I stare at her, waiting for an answer to the question I can't bring myself to ask.

"No. No, my dear, no one took me. No one would've dared to take me. My parents had the entire town—the entire country—looking for me at one point, but they couldn't find someone who didn't want to be found."

"But why?" I demand.

"The why doesn't matter nearly as much as the how, now does it? And you've just discovered my how." She gestures around the room.

"You've just been, what, hiding out in the walls all this time? For thirty years? How is that even possible? How did you find this place?"

"Well, that was just luck, really," she says, her smile growing proud. "Initially, right after I killed him, I ran away. As far as I could. I left the state and hid out in a motel, where I could watch the investigation as it went on and make sure they weren't on my trail. But...well, you know what they say. Criminals like to return to the scene of the crime. Once things had calmed down, I came back. I just planned to see the place, but these teenagers broke in and I had to run and hide in the attic. I'd always been afraid of going up there."

She sighs. "This house is old. There were all sorts of servants' entrances and hidden passages. One to nearly every room, as it turns out. It was then I realized no one was looking for me anymore. I could just live here in the walls. Forever, if I wanted to. No one would know."

Something Tennessee said earlier floats through my mind. Something about teenagers trying to stay here overnight, and how they'd hear footsteps and a baby crying.

"And your son? You kept him with you?" It all makes sense.

She laughs under her breath. "My dear, you really have done your homework, haven't you?"

"He's been helping you all this time, hasn't he?" I piece it together as I speak. "It's... Your son is Daniel, isn't it?"

A smile grows on her thin lips, and she says with a sneer, "Now, that's the first time you've been wrong all night." She clicks her tongue with disapproval. "He's too old to be mine. I know I don't look great after all these years in the walls, but give me some credit. I'm not *ancient*."

The hope in my chest fades. She's right. Their ages don't line up. "But then who... That only leaves..." I cast a terrified glance at Tennessee, who stares back at me, shaking his head with wild eyes.

"No, Blakely, I—"

Lessa interrupts him with a scoff. "I was in no state to raise a baby after everything that happened, but my parents were. They could take care of my Isaac like I couldn't. I

202

couldn't go back to my old life, to my family, not with everyone looking for me. I didn't even know if they'd want me back after everything I did, but the least any of us could do was make sure he was taken care of. My parents weren't perfect, but I had a good life with them. Their staff took good care of me. I was safe and healthy and, in a world like this, sometimes that's all you can ask for. And, from here, I could check in on Isaac from time to time."

"You...you gave him away? Let your parents raise him?" It doesn't add up. "If that's true, then, what about the rumors? People said they heard a baby crying here. What baby? Was that all made up?"

Her grin grows stiff, but she doesn't answer straight away.

"Why are we here?" Tennessee asks, getting back to business. "What do you want from us?"

She folds her hands together in front of her stomach. "It's simple, really. I need your help."

"Help?" Lyra scoffs. "Hell of a way to get it from us. Why would we help you after all you've done?"

"Oh, I'm sorry." She giggles, her fingers flying to her mouth. "It seems I've given you the impression I'm going to ask for your help, rather than take it."

Tennessee grips my wrist.

"This place was my home. It wasn't anything special, but it was mine. The only thing that had ever been mine without my parents' help. I fought for it. Killed for it, even." Her voice goes feral. "I *deserved* this house."

She pauses, huffing, and seems to collect herself. "It was the best way for me to stay close enough to watch my son grow up and, once the police had stopped looking for me, it was the perfect place to hide. No one would ever look for me here. Or anywhere in this town, for that matter. And I would've been content to live out the rest of my days here. Not bothering anyone else. But then, as luck would have it, the news came that someone had bought the place. They wanted to make it into a dreadful little writer's retreat, which was...ironic, at best."

She doesn't elaborate on what seems like an inside joke. "But then, I had the idea to use their little plan to my benefit. You see... I'm old and sick. I don't have much time left. I had to come up with a plan, and fast, in order to help someone I care about. This story...the story of four of the world's most famous writers, trapped in a house with a sordid past, picked off one by one... Well, to be frank, it's the story of a lifetime. The *payday* of a lifetime. All we had to do was take out the office employees, send emails to make sure no one else would interrupt our little plan, and then invite you all here."

"What are you talking about?" Tennessee demands.

"Four..." I press my fingers to my temples as my brain pounds with threats of blacking out.

"What?" He checks on me over his shoulder.

"She said four," Lyra confirms, nodding at me. "*Four* of the world's most famous writers. Not five."

I cut a look at Lucy. "There was another baby, wasn't there? Living here with you."

"You really are smart, Blakely. Pity your novels don't show it." She clicks her tongue.

"You were pregnant when you killed him. Your husband." I stare into space, trying to make it all fit in my head. "And that baby was one of us... It was..." I gasp as it clicks, just as she comes into view, her body coated with more of the fake blood.

"Aidy?" The weight of the betrayal is apparent in Lyra's voice.

"You tricked us," Tennessee says through gritted teeth.

"You've been behind it all, haven't you? The missing items, the... Did you kill those people at the office?"

She shakes her head. "Mom took care of them when it was time. I'm no murderer. Don't quite have it in me. Isn't that right, Tennessee?"

"What?" he asks, his jaw slack.

"That's what you said about the book I wrote. Our publisher wanted you to blurb it, and your review was scathing." She puts on a voice that's meant to sound like Tennessee. "This author's stories are better suited to puppies and rainbows than hard-boiled thrillers. A promising premise, but the execution is as interesting as watching paint dry."

"Wait, wait, wait, is that what this is about? Because I gave you a bad review?"

"Not just you," she says firmly. "*All* of you. Every single one of you tore my debut to shreds. My career was over before it began." She shakes her head. "I had to rebrand as a cozy author under this ridiculous pen name."

"That's no reason to do this, Aidy," Lyra says, her voice soft. "We're sorry if we hurt your feelings. Every one of us gets bad reviews. They all cut just the same, but it's part of it. You ignore them and move on."

"Oh, so I was just supposed to ignore four titans of our industry telling me I should never write again? Telling me I'd never be good enough to make it in *their world?*" She shoves her fists into her hips.

"Well, obviously you proved us wrong," I say. "I'm really sorry, Aidy. But, please, whatever you're planning, please just let us go. You don't have to do this."

"Where's Daniel?" Tennessee asks. "Is he part of this too? You said we all wrote you bad reviews. Did you do something to him?"

"The plan was to take you out one by one tonight, the anniversary of my father's murder, but Daniel found one of the doorways early. He snuck up on Mom while Lyra and I were with the police. She did what she had to do."

"What? You...you killed him?" I take a step back, feeling dizzy.

Neither of them answers.

"How've you been getting in and out? We saw you outside. You were covered in blood..." Tennessee's words come slower as he figures it out, just like I have. "The bunker. It leads inside the house, doesn't it?"

"The tunnel leads to a set of stairs that bring you up into the walls on the bottom floor," Aidy tells us. "From there, you can get anywhere in the house if you know the way."

"But why? What are you going to gain from this? A payday, like your mom said? Do you really believe that will work?" he asks.

"I know it will." She certainly sounds sure. "Think about it. A serial killer returns to the scene of the crime after thirty years and picks off some of the most famous writers of our generation. I'm the sole survivor. The only one left to share our story." She smiles. "Don't worry. *I'll make you all look really good.*"

The phrase causes something in the back of my mind to resurface. As the memory hits me, I feel myself beginning to fade.

Then, darkness finds me.

Just like that, I'm gone.

CHAPTER THIRTY-ONE

BLAKELY

BEFORE

"You look beautiful. Stop worrying." Theo puts his hand over mine on the tabletop, offering a kind smile. Even in the most stressful situations, he always manages to be calm. I'll never understand it.

"Momma, can I get another ice cream?" Oliver asks, looking up at me with a white mustache.

I pass him a cloth napkin. "Wipe your mouth, please. And no, I think that's enough ice cream for one night. Mommy's speech is coming up soon."

"And she's going to do so well," Theo says, grinning at me from across the table.

"If I don't trip up the stairs."

"You'll do fi—"

"Oh my god, Blakely Baldwin!"

I turn to see a woman coming toward me. She has long, brown hair with short bangs and is dressed in a floral-patterned jumpsuit with a fanny pack around her hips. She holds out her arms, expecting me to hug her, and I do so awkwardly from my seat.

"Sorry, I'm a hugger. I'm such a huge fan," she says. "I loved your last one about the two sisters…"

"*The Last Secret?* Oh, thanks!" I beam.

"What are you working on now?"

"I'm between books right now, just trying to find inspiration. Are you… Are you a writer?"

"Oh." A pink blush creeps to her cheeks. "Yeah, but nothing you would've read. I'm Aidy Moreau. I write cozies."

"Nothing wrong with that. My grandma loved cozies."

Her smile is stiff, but she recovers quickly. I hadn't meant for it to be an insult, but it seems she took it that way. "You're giving a speech tonight, aren't you?"

"Yeah, the keynote," I tell her, a hint of pride in my words. "I've been attending this conference for years, so it's pretty exciting to be honored like this."

"I'd say! Congratulations. Oh, let me fix your hair just a bit." She brushes her fingers through it without permission. "You've got a few flyaways. Don't worry… I'll make sure you look good before you go up there. Us girls gotta stick together." She winks at me.

I swallow, sitting silently as she adjusts my hair.

When she's done, she says, "Hey, listen, I won't take up too much of your time, but I wanted to buy you a drink to say congratulations."

I smile. "Oh, you don't have to do that."

She points to the wineglass on my table. "Cabernet?"

"Yes, that's great."

"Be right back."

She stands, waving her fingers at Oliver before walking away from the table.

"Well, that was nice," Theo says.

"Yeah, I guess so. Although, I probably shouldn't have any more to drink if I want to have my head on straight while I give the speech."

"You've only had one glass," he says.

"I know. You can have it if you want."

Aidy returns to the table moments later and hands me a glass of wine. "Here you go."

"Thank you so much again, Aidy. It was great to meet you." I place the glass down on the table.

She stands there for a second, watching me, but after a few awkward moments of silence pass, she bounces up on her toes with an exaggerated shrug. "I'll see you later. Good luck up there!"

I trace a finger along the condensation of the glass, knees bouncing with nerves. When I look up, I spot my best friend coming through the door. "There's Katy and Noah!" I shoot up from the table and wave them toward us. "*Over here!*" I whisper-shout.

"Hey. Oh my god, you look stunning. What a babe." She hugs me as Noah shakes Theo's hand and pats Oliver's head.

"Here, sit." I let them slide into the booth between Theo and me.

Katy gives a playful look to Oliver. "You're out past your bedtime, Little Man."

He licks his spoon. "Momma says it's okay tonight 'cause she's *keysnote person.*"

"Keynote speaker," I say with an encouraging nod.

"Where's Kara?" he asks Katy.

"Kara is with her *Lola* and *Lolo*," Katy says. "It was also past her bedtime." She winks at me.

"We're just staying for Blakely's speech. Then I'm taking Little Man home and we're leaving Mommy to mingle."

"Want us to take him so you can stay and schmooze with your wifey?" Katy asks. "If I were you, I wouldn't leave her alone in this dress."

Theo grins proudly. "Nah, trust me, I don't want to, but I promised Ollie I'd read him a new book before bed tonight. It just arrived today. Thanks, though."

"And I won't be out long anyway," I add. "Just an hour or so to do pictures at the end of the ceremony. It's been a long day." As if to prove a point, I release a loud yawn.

"As evidenced by the wineglass you haven't touched." Noah points to it.

"I know. I shouldn't have gotten it. I don't want to drink any more before I go up on stage, and it'll be warm by the time my speech is over." I push it toward Theo as the lights go down. "You have it. I don't want it to go to waste."

He takes a sip as the ceremony starts, and I wring my hands in my lap under the table, reciting my speech over and over again in my head until they call my name.

I don't remember most of what I said by the end of it, still riding the adrenaline high. I kiss Theo and Ollie before they head out, and I sit through the rest of the ceremony feeling relieved that it's over.

When the ceremony ends and the lights come up, I have three missed calls from Theo and a voice mail, but it's not his voice on the line.

"There's been an accident," the officer tells me.

I don't remember much else about that night. Except that it's the night I lost everything.

A FEW MONTHS LATER, the news broke that my husband had been drinking before the crash that ended both his and my son's lives. I didn't know what to make of it. He'd had the glass of wine, sure, but that was it. Neither Katy nor Noah recalled him drinking any more while I was on stage. Whatever he'd had, it wasn't enough to make him inebriated. Theo was cautious. He'd never have been so reckless.

One glass was always his limit when he drove, but that night, though his blood alcohol level wasn't above the legal limit, it was still high. Too high to have been driving.

It didn't make sense. I knew my husband. Knew he'd never put Ollie in danger like that, but no matter what I said, no matter what I told the police, no one listened.

Once the news had spread, everyone had an opinion. And suddenly, my tragedy was the talk of the town. People discussed it on their social media pages, old friends reached out to *lend an ear,* and suddenly, I was the woman who'd been married to the alcoholic who'd killed my son.

And, try as I might to move on from it, to forgive Theo, to forgive myself for handing him what I had believed was the drink that set him over the limit, there was no escaping the fact that I could never look back on what should've been one of the greatest nights of my life without remembering the worst.

CHAPTER THIRTY-TWO

PRESENT DAY

Her words ring in my head. *I'll make you look good.*

It was what she'd said about my hair that night, and what she said about the book just then. When I come to, Tennessee is standing in front of me and Lucy has the gun held out, pointed directly at him.

"You don't have to do this," he says calmly, his hands in the air.

The weight of the realization crushes me. How could I not have seen it before? I recall what Lyra said earlier, about the rumors that someone had spiked the drinks. All the speakers except one. *Mine.*

Unless...

"You put something in my drink that night, didn't you?" I ask, sitting up. Why didn't I see it? Why didn't I question it?

Those months were a blur of rage, anger, and grief, but

it's no excuse. I should've fought harder for him. Should've been more determined to learn the truth.

It's what one of my characters would've done.

It's what a good wife—a good mother—would do.

A weight settles in my gut when Aidy looks at me.

"What are you talking about?" Lucy asks.

"The drink you brought me, I gave it to my husband, and he died that night. My son..." My voice cracks. A bitter loathing snakes its way through my core, up my spine, and through my extremities. Problem is, I can't tell whom I loathe more—Aidy or myself. How could I be so blind? The truth was right in front of me all along. "They said he had been drinking too much, but I knew it wasn't true. It wasn't until just now I realized... You put something in the drink you gave me, didn't you?"

Aidy's still. She frowns. "I gave *you* the drink. I had no control over what you did with it."

Furious, I leap to my feet. "*They called him a drunk.* A murderer. They said awful, awful things about him...but I knew better. I knew better, and still, I questioned it." I'm ashamed to admit it.

"Sucks how much words hurt, doesn't it?" Aidy sneers, unaffected by anything I'm saying.

"They were innocent," I bellow. Lucy lifts the gun to point at me, but Tennessee moves in front of me again.

In what feels like slow motion, I blink, realizing what has to be done.

"If you'll all be still, we'll make this as painless as possible," Lucy says.

"I'm dying." I squeeze my eyes shut as the admission comes out.

"What?" Every eye in the room falls to me.

"I have a brain tumor. It's inoperable. It's..." My eyes find Tennessee's in the darkness. "It's why I black out when I get stressed. They found it a few months ago. I came here to write my final book. The book I want to be remembered by. But...the truth is, since losing them, I don't care about writing anymore. I don't care about anything."

He opens his mouth to speak, but I step forward, gripping his hand firmly, trying to say all I need to say without the words to say it. I lean forward, pressing my lips to his cheek so I'm close enough to whisper, "Three against two. I'm dying anyway. Don't let them win." Without giving him the chance to object, I squeeze his arm, turn, and lunge.

"Blakely, no!"

What happens next comes in a blur of screams and gunshots. I throw my body forward just as white-hot pain tears through me. I land on Lucy, and she crumples to the ground with me on top. I should be able to do something, but I can't move. I cradle my hands over my stomach, trying to soothe the pain as I feel someone pulling me off of her.

Someone screams.

"Tennessee!"

Thud.

Thud.

Thud.

Bang.

"Fuck!"

Another scream.

Arms cradle me. Someone is holding me.

I'm shoved to the side.

The world goes black.

When I wake, I'm face down on the floor. *How did I get here?* I spy the gun just inches from me. I reach a finger out, trying to grab it.

Crunch.

Aidy's foot comes down on my fingers. She twists her heel into my bones, and I cry out. At least, I think I do. I can't be sure of anything right now.

In seconds, she stumbles. Someone knocks her to the ground.

"Blakely, can you hear me?"

Two hands grab me, and they're pulling me away. It's Tennessee... Or maybe Theo? Is Theo here? Did he bring Ollie?

Am I dreaming?

Is this my nightmare?

I'm dragged against the wood floor by someone I can't see.

Bang.

Another scream.

The darkness comes for me quickly and, for once, I welcome it.

CHAPTER THIRTY-THREE

ONE YEAR LATER

"And that's basically it," Lyra says, staring across the table at the men and women dressed in suits. "Lessa shot Blakely, and it was enough of a distraction for me to knock Aidy out while Tennessee fought to get the gun away from Lessa. It was a struggle, and we didn't leave unscathed, obviously. It all happened so quickly. We're lucky to have gotten out with our lives, but we did."

She reaches out and grips my hand. I nod, smiling back at her. It's been painful to recount everything that happened, but together, we made it through.

"And is it true? Do you really have a brain tumor?" the first man asks with absolutely zero tact.

"I do. My doctor is trying an experimental drug. It's gotten pretty good results in clinical trials so far. At this point, every single day is another day they told me I wouldn't have."

Tennessee grips my leg under the table.

"And why was the shower turned on in the bathroom? When you thought Lyra was in there? I don't think that was ever explained?"

"We think Aidy was trying to scare us by drawing our attention that way. Obviously, we haven't been able to find out, but the police seem to agree. There was a water shut off on the other side of that wall. If she was trying to distract us from finding Lyra, it certainly worked," I say with a shrug. "Honestly, a lot of what they did, like breaking the hot tub, if that's what happened, seemed like it was either to worry or scare us, or to try to turn us against each other."

Lyra pins me with a playful sideways glance. "Which actually worked."

One of the men leans forward, looking at Tennessee. "And you found everything in the walls of that house after it happened? Laptops, phones, everything?"

"There are plenty of police photos to prove it," Tennessee says. "We used Aidy's phone to call them as soon as it was safe to do so, as well as an ambulance for Blakely. We found all of our things, as well as evidence they'd been living there for years."

"And Dan's body, of course," I say. We all look down solemnly.

"We'd actually like to dedicate the book to his memory," Lyra says. "We think it would be a good way to remember him."

"We agree," the woman at the head of the table says. "It sounds like this story could be the thing that makes each of your careers. I know you're focused on fiction, but this story...it's the story of a lifetime. Your best work, maybe ever.

With the marketing campaign we'll put in place, this will make you all household names."

We exchange glances.

It won't bring them back. Won't make any of it okay. But it's all we can do.

It's the last story I'll ever write, and the one I want to seal my legacy and clear my husband's name.

I meet Lyra's eyes and she nods at me, a clear answer. Then, we turn to Tennessee, who nods too. With that, I lean forward, extending my hand. The woman at the head of the table reaches out to accept it. "I think we have a deal."

A YEAR AND A HALF LATER, I'm staring at the book the three of us have spent the last year writing. The one we'll spend the next nine months promoting while on tour.

The doctors are feeling positive about my prognosis. I have maybe five years left, but each day is a gift. It's more than I should've had.

Tennessee walks into the room, a mug of tea in his hand, cat at his feet. There are boxes of my things throughout his apartment that still need to be unpacked, but if there's anything we've learned through all of this, it's that we want to spend our time doing what we love.

The boxes can wait.

We sink into the couch, holding the first copy of the new book.

I open it, reading it aloud to him.

"*A Quiet Retreat*, by Lyra James, Blakely Baldwin, and Tennessee Rivers. To Daniel, for inspiring us in every way.

May your memory forever live on in these pages and in every page you've written."

My voice cracks and I pause, collecting myself as I feel his thumb rubbing rhythmic circles on my shoulder.

"From Lyra: To my aunties, for preparing me for this crazy life. To my wife, for telling me to get home safe. To my daughters, for being my reasons for everything."

I smile at him over my shoulder. "From Tennessee: To my mom, for teaching me to stand up for what's right. To my niece and nephews, for always making me laugh. And to Blakely Baldwin, for loving me more every day and teaching me it's okay for the women to save themselves."

He kisses my temple, and I close my eyes, soaking in the moment before reading the final piece of the dedication. "From Blakely: To Theo and Oliver, for trusting me enough to deliver your truth. To Tennessee, for making me believe there's a reason to fight again. And to Aidy, for everything you stole from me and everything I'm taking back. In the end, you kept your word. Thanks for making me look good."

ENJOYED A QUIET RETREAT?

If you enjoyed this story, please consider leaving me a quick review. It doesn't have to be long—just a few words will do. Who knows? Your review might be the thing that encourages a future reader to take a chance on my work!
To leave a review, please visit:
https://mybook.to/aquietretreat

Let everyone know how much you loved
A Quiet Retreat on Goodreads:
https://bit.ly/3T6S3rJ

STAY UP TO DATE ON EVERYTHING KMOD!

Thank you so much for reading this story. I'd love to invite you to sign up for my mailing list and text alerts so we can be sure you don't miss my next release.

Sign up for my mailing list here:
kierstenmodglinauthor.com/nlsignup

Sign up for my text alerts here:
kierstenmodglinauthor.com/textalerts

ACKNOWLEDGMENTS

First and foremost, to my husband and sweet little girl—thank you for loving me, for believing in me, and for standing beside me through all the highs and lows. I love you both more than I could ever put into words.

To my bestie, Emerald O'Brien—thank you for our chats, the inspiration you give me, for always having the perfect solution to any problem, and for being the most selfless, encouraging person I know. I love you, friend. So, so grateful for you.

To my immensely talented editor, Sarah West—thank you for your belief in my stories and characters. Thank you for trusting the story I'm trying to tell and helping me find it through all the chaos of my first drafts. I'm so thankful to have you on my team.

To the proofreading team at My Brother's Editor, Rosa and Ellie—thank you for being the final set of eyes on my stories and for knowing all the grammar rules (like ALLLLLL of them. Seriously, don't your brains hurt?!). I wouldn't trust anyone else with my final drafts. I'm incredibly appreciative of all you do for me.

To my loyal readers (AKA the #KMod Squad)—I can't put into words what you guys mean to me. I'm so incredibly thankful for your support, for your belief in me, and for your unending excitement for each new story. Thank you for always being ready to celebrate the highs with me, for cheering me on, for leaving reviews, shouting out recommendations to your friends and families, and for always, always, always being in my corner. I love you and couldn't do this without you.

To my book club/gang/besties—Sara, both Erins, June, Heather, Dee, and Rhonda—my girls! Thank you so much for all the laughs (and the cries), the brainstorming sessions, and the amazing support you've given me. I'm so grateful for your friendship, for our Wednesday nights, for the book club trips, for every time Sara tells us she has a *special surprise* for us and we're just waiting to see what costume she'll show up wearing, and everything else in between. I love you, girls!

To my writing friends—Emerald O'Brien (again!), Leigh M. Hall, Adriane Leigh, Rachel Renee, Kate Gable, AJ Campbell, Melissa Grace, AJ Wills, AJ McDine, Lynessa Layne, Katie Blanchard, Carrie Magillen, Kelly Utt, LP Snyder, Kirstie Goode, Wendy Owens, Drew Strickland, Amanda J. Clay, Elana Johnson, Siera London, Alessandra Torre, Lauren Griffey, Craig Martelle, Mariah Kingsley, Laura Kemp, Nola Nash, Lisa Regan, Kat Shehata, Hillary DeVisser, Lauren Lee, Lena Derhally, Cora Kenborn, and SO many others—thank you for being who you are. Thank you for making the publishing industry better, kinder, and more welcoming. I love you guys!

To Becca and Lexy—thank you for keeping things running when I can't come up for air. You guys have been one of the best parts of my 2022 and I'm very, very thankful for you.

To Lessa Gregg, a sweet reader who let me borrow her

name for this story—thank you for trusting me with it. I hope you enjoyed meeting Lessa!

Last but certainly not least, to you—thank you for purchasing this book and supporting my dream. I'm so grateful that you took a chance on Blakely's story and I truly hope you enjoyed reading it. Whether this is your first Kiersten Modglin book or your 35th, I hope it was everything you wished for and nothing like you expected!

ABOUT THE AUTHOR

KIERSTEN MODGLIN is an Amazon Top 10 bestselling author of psychological thrillers and a member of International Thriller Writers, Novelists, Inc., and the Alliance of Independent Authors. Kiersten is a KDP Select All-Star and a recipient of *ThrillerFix's* Best Psychological Thriller Award, *Suspense Magazine's* Best Book of 2021 Award, a 2022 Silver Falchion for Best Suspense, and a 2022 Silver Falchion for Best Overall Book of 2021. She grew up in rural western Kentucky and later relocated to Nashville, Tennessee, where she now lives with her husband, daughter, and their two Boston terriers: Cedric and Georgie. Kiersten's work is currently being translated into multiple languages and readers across the world refer to her as 'The Queen of Twists.' A Netflix addict, Shonda Rhimes superfan, psychology fanatic, and *indoor* enthusiast, Kiersten enjoys rainy days spent with her nose in a book.

Sign up for Kiersten's newsletter here:
kierstenmodglinauthor.com/nlsignup

Sign up for text alerts from Kiersten here:
kierstenmodglinauthor.com/textalerts

kierstenmodglinauthor.com
www.facebook.com/kierstenmodglinauthor
www.facebook.com/groups/kmodsquad
www.twitter.com/kmodglinauthor
www.instagram.com/kierstenmodglinauthor
www.tiktok.com/@kierstenmodglinauthor
www.goodreads.com/kierstenmodglinauthor
www.bookbub.com/authors/kiersten-modglin
www.amazon.com/author/kierstenmodglin

ALSO BY KIERSTEN MODGLIN

STANDALONE NOVELS

Becoming Mrs. Abbott

The List

The Missing Piece

Playing Jenna

The Beginning After

The Better Choice

The Good Neighbors

The Lucky Ones

I Said Yes

The Mother-in-Law

The Dream Job

The Nanny's Secret

The Liar's Wife

My Husband's Secret

The Perfect Getaway

The Roommate

The Missing

Just Married

Our Little Secret

Widow Falls

Missing Daughter

The Reunion

Tell Me the Truth

The Dinner Guests

If You're Reading This...

ARRANGEMENT TRILOGY

The Arrangement (Book 1)

The Amendment (Book 2)

The Atonement (Book 3)

THE MESSES SERIES

The Cleaner (The Messes, #1)

The Healer (The Messes, #2)

The Liar (The Messes, #3)

The Prisoner (The Messes, #4)

NOVELLAS

The Long Route: A Lover's Landing Novella

The Stranger in the Woods: A Crimson Falls Novella